*A
Harlequin
Romance*

CHARLOTTE'S HURRICANE

by

ANNE MATHER

HARLEQUIN BOOKS

Toronto • Canada   New York • New York

CHARLOTTE'S HURRICANE

First published in 1970 by Mills & Boon Limited,
17-19 Foley Street, London, England.

Harlequin Canadian edition published April, 1971
Harlequin U.S. edition published July, 1971

Standard Book Number: 373-51487-5.

Printed in Canada

CHAPTER ONE

In the hotel lounge several fans stirred the languid air, causing a faint breeze, but barely cooling the temperature. At this hour of the afternoon the whole population of the island seemed to be asleep and even the yellow hibiscus, swaying on its lattice framework, had a somnolent air. The cane chairs were empty now, and the barefoot Indian boys who worked so energetically during the latter hours of the day, providing chinking iced drinks for the guests, seemed all to have melted away for their siesta.

But Charlotte was not used to sleeping away the afternoon, and as she was young and healthy, she saw no reason to prolong her stay in the bedroom, which while being of generous proportions nevertheless had a claustrophobic atmosphere in this enervating heat. It was her first experience of the tropics, and as yet not even the heat could quell her natural excitement and enthusiasm. She wanted to go out and explore, but a girl alone was an obvious target in an alien port, and although the Fijians seemed friendly people, she was loath to leave the hotel without an escort. Besides, there was still the possibility that Andrew Meredith might try to get in touch with her.

She sighed and crossing the empty lounge seated herself in a cane lounger on the verandah, from where she could see below her the harbour with its timbered wharves, the stalls of the vegetable market overflowing on to the surrounding roads. There were ships in the harbour of all shapes and sizes, from a huge passenger liner to the small copra coasters that

5

plied between the smaller islands collecting the sacks of dried copra and supplying necessary stores.

The brilliance of the vegetation that surrounded the hotel and which grew in such abundance all over Viti Levu hurt her eyes, and she was glad she had remembered to put dark glasses into the pocket of her cotton pants. Sliding them on to her nose, she surveyed the scene in more detail, wondering what she would do if Andrew Meredith failed to get in touch with her. Evan was relying on her to keep this appointment, and although she had no authority to make any actual decisions on the agency's behalf, she was perfectly capable of visiting the island involved, and assessing its qualities, so that when Evan was able to join her she would have all the facts at her fingertips.

It was annoying that Evan had been unable to accompany her as originally planned. After all, she was only his assistant, and although this trip to Polynesia had all the trappings of a holiday, it was not meant to be. Charlotte would not have been human if she had not appreciated the excitement of it all, but she was conscious of her responsibilities, and she could not lie around the hotel indefinitely waiting for this Meredith man to contact her. She supposed she ought to have cabled Evan when Andrew Meredith did not meet her at the International airport at Nandi, as arranged, but with all his other worries, she had not wanted to trouble him. And now here she was in Suva two days later, and still without any word from Meredith.

The hotel manager had been very kind, but as Manatoa was a small island, far out in the Fijian group, without efficient means of communication, there was little he could suggest.

Drawing out a packet of cigarettes, Charlotte put one between her lips and lit it slowly, savouring the relaxation it engendered. If Evan had been here, it would have been his worry, and she would have felt free to relax, but as it was it all rested on her shoulders, and she just didn't know what to do next.

Hearing a sound behind her, she glanced round in time to see the hotel manager approaching. A beaming smile enveloped his dusky face, and Charlotte felt that faint feeling of expectancy one experiences when one believes something is about to happen.

The manager was a big man, broad and muscular, like many of the Fijians Charlotte had seen, and for all that she was a tall girl, he dwarfed her with his bulk. Swinging her slender legs to the ground, she rose to her feet, as he said:

"Ah, Miss Carlisle! I thought I might find you here. I have some good news for you."

Charlotte's eyes widened. "You've heard from Mr. Meredith?"

The manager shook his head. "No, not that. But maybe something just as good."

Charlotte wondered. What else was there?

The burly Fijian indicated her lounger. "Won't you sit down again, Miss Carlisle, and perhaps you will allow me to offer you a glass of iced lime?"

Charlotte was consumed with impatience, but she managed a smile, and subsided back on to her chair, while the manager crossed the room to the bar and helped himself from the refrigerated cabinet. Then he returned with two glasses, and after she had accepted hers and sipped it gratefully, he seated himself opposite her.

"Now," he said, obviously enjoying her suspense, "I have this afternoon been talking to a Captain

Koroledo, who owns a copra ship, lying in the harbour at this moment. It was quite by chance that I learned that his ships calls at Manatoa."

Charlotte felt a quivering sensation in the pit of her stomach. "Oh, yes?" she said, rather doubtfully.

"Yes. It occurred to me that had Mr. Meredith been in Suva, he would have heard by now that you were here. Besides, this was the hotel where he had booked accommodation, was it not?"

"Of course."

"So it is reasonable to assume that Mr. Meredith has been delayed for some unavoidable reason, and therefore your best plan would be to go to Manatoa and visit Meredith there."

Charlotte swallowed hard. "You—you're suggesting I travel on—on this copra vessel?"

"Of course. That is what Mr. Hunter would have done, is it not?"

Charlotte sighed. Indeed yes, that was exactly what Evan would have done. But Evan was a man, and she was not. She compressed her lips. This was just the kind of situation she had always deplored— that where her sex became of more importance than her intelligence.

Fingering the rim of her glass, she said tentatively: "When—when does this copra ship leave?"

"Tonight—quite late, I believe."

Charlotte raised her dark eyebrows. "I see. And —er—when will it reach Manatoa?"

The manager grinned, his teeth very white against his black skin. "In two days. Captain Koroledo expects to reach Manatoa on Friday."

Charlotte gasped. Two days! Aboard a copra ship!

Although her nostrils were becoming slightly adjusted to the pungent, sickly smell of copra, she could not imagine herself surviving two whole days, or perhaps longer, actually living alongside such a cargo. She was quite sure that was the reason the manager was grinning so broadly. He didn't think she would be able to do it either.

Stiffening her shoulders, she said: "I didn't know those ships took passengers."

"Oh, yes, they take passengers. The accommodation is sometimes primitive, but the ships are solid enough."

Charlotte stubbed out her cigarette. This was a challenge, of course, and she had never been able to resist a challenge. But on the other hand, she was not in England now, she was in Fiji, and the chances were that she would be the only woman on the vessel, certainly the only white woman.

The manager was sitting watching the display of shifting emotions that were evident in her expression, and it was obvious that he didn't expect her to go. After all, she argued with herself, there was no guarantee that Andrew Meredith would be waiting for her at Manatoa. Maybe his reasons for not arriving at Nandi were of a different nature. Maybe he had had difficulties with his own transport, and perhaps he was even now waiting at some out of the way quayside for a ship to bring him to meet her.

She sighed again, and moved out of her chair to the verandah rail, looking down on the harbour, as though trying to distinguish Captain Koroledo's vessel from all the others anchored there.

Swinging round, she said: "Did—did you make any arrangements with Captain Koroledo?"

The manager shook his head. "Of course not, Miss Carlisle. Naturally I wanted to discuss it with you first."

Charlotte lifted her shoulders in an indecisive gesture. "I wish I knew what to do. What if I get there and Mr. Meredith isn't there?"

The manager shrugged his broad shoulders. "You could return with the copra ship, of course."

Charlotte hesitated. "Yes, I could do that, couldn't I?"

The manager nodded. He rose to his feet. "I must go, Miss Carlisle, there are other matters needing my attention. I understand that you will need time to think over such a decision. I will come back later, and if you have decided to go, I will make the necessary arrangements with Captain Koroledo myself."

"Thank you."

After he had gone, Charlotte lit another cigarette, nervously aware that she was smoking too much, but that was really all it was—nerves. She walked about the verandah restlessly, unable to sit and think about such an expedition. Then, with rivulets of sweat running down her back, she had to sit down to cool down. Even on the verandah the air was humid, and she fanned herself with a mat from the glass-topped table.

If only Evan were nearer so that she could get on the telephone and ask him his opinion! But she could hardly expect to make a call to London from here, and even if she could, she knew in her heart of hearts that Evan would not approve. Although he treated her as his equal in her work, this was something completely different, and he was old-fashioned enough to believe that as a woman she ought to behave with some degree of decorum.

Deciding that she might be able to think more clearly after a refreshing shower, Charlotte rose from her seat on the verandah, and crossing the lounge again, took the lift up to her room. In the adjoining bathroom, she stripped off her clothes and turned on the cold tap of the shower. The shock of the icy water against her hot skin caused her to gasp breathlessly for a moment, and then as she got used to it a healthy tingling sensation removed all the inertia the heat of the afternoon had aroused. She dressed in a slim shift of blue cotton, combed her long hair into a knot on top of her head, and applied a pale lipstick to her lips. Then she walked on to her balcony and leaned on the rail thoughtfully.

Her room overlooked the swimming pool at the rear of the hotel, which was gradually coming to life as the heat of the afternoon was passing. She had already sampled the delights of the pool that morning, before most of the hotel's guests were even awake.

Now her thoughts were not on the pool, or its sun-bronzed inhabitants. She was still wrapped up with her own problems. Deep down inside she knew that she could not refuse the chance to possibly contact Andrew Meredith and it was annoying to realize that the only reason she showed any outward hesitation was because of the vulnerability of being a woman. If Evan had dreamed that Meredith would not be at Nandi to meet her, as planned, she would never have been allowed out of the country.

Last year, when she handled the Austrian deal for him, had been different. Then, she was only an hour's flying time away from London, with free access by

11

telephone. But here, thousands of miles from England, in a country which while being a British Colony was nevertheless wholly alien to her, she was in danger of losing some of her confidence.

And that would never do! She was Evan Hunter's personal assistant, a position which she had worked hard to achieve, and she could not—she *would* not jeopardize this deal, just because of her sex. After all, if she could see the island, and approve in principle this man Meredith's terms, Evan would have to agree that she had done the right thing. And if Meredith were not on Manatoa after all, there was no harm done. She could return, as the hotel manager had said, with the copra ship, and if it meant she must suffer the smell of the copra for a week or so, then what of it? She had never been prone to nausea, and the fact that she was already getting used to the smell proved that one could forget about it, given time.

The decision made, she heaved a sigh and walked back into her bedroom. If she was leaving tonight she ought to make some effort to pack a few clothes. Obviously she would not be able to take very much, but at the outside she should be away only a few days, and during that time slacks and shirts and perhaps one dress for evening wear would suffice. Luckily most of her clothes were uncrushable and would push into her canvas holdall.

Then she used the hotel telephone and rang the manager to tell him of her decision. If he was surprised that she should have decided to go after all, he managed to conceal it, and agreed to make the necessary arrangements with Captain Koroledo.

She had dinner in the hotel dining room quite early so as to give herself plenty of time to change afterwards. The manager approached her as she was having coffee after the meal, and asked whether he might join her.

"Of course," exclaimed Charlotte, smiling. "Sit down. Have you seen Captain Koroledo?"

"Yes, Miss Carlisle, I've spoken to him. He is quite happy to take you as a passenger, and moreover, he knows this Mr. Meredith."

"Does he?" Charlotte's eyes widened excitedly. At last, it seemed, luck was returning to her.

"Yes. The ship is called the *Fijian Star* and she leaves this evening at nine-thirty, in—let me see"— he consulted his wrist watch—"in exactly one hour. Can you be ready in about half an hour, and I will take you down to meet him?"

Charlotte felt the now familiar quivers of excitement running along her veins. "I—I have packed," she said, nodding. "I have only to change into something more suitable."

"Very well, I will be waiting. And now, if you will excuse me . . ." He rose again, and as Charlotte nodded, he walked away.

"Well, Charlotte," she said to herself, a trifle tremulously, "you're almost on your way!"

The *Fijian Star* was a vessel of some two hundred tons, operating a service for the plantation owners of the outer islands. It could not have been called elegant by any stretch of the imagination, and smelt overpoweringly of its usual cargo. Charlotte half doubted its seaworthiness, and then decided that if she allowed thoughts of that kind to invade her mind, she would never survive the voyage.

Captain Koroledo was a giant of a man, bigger even than the hotel manager, with a mass of dark hair

13

that encroached down his cheeks and ended in a black beard. His rather piratical appearance was tempered by twinkling eyes below bushy brows, and a wide and charming grin. His only concession to formality was the peaked cap he wore to denote his rank of captain, but his crew members wore a variety of garments, mostly leaving muscular chests bare.

Unfortunately, or so Charlotte at first felt, there were to be no other passengers this trip, but Captain Koroledo quickly changed her mind when he revealed that there was no actual accommodation for passengers, but in the circumstances, as she was the only passenger, he was allowing her to use his cabin.

The Captain's cabin proved to be a very workmanlike room, with a broad framework strewn with maps, charts and weather information taking up most of the space. The linen on the bunk was sparkling white, however, and a tiny alcove provided the means for a shower of sea-water if so desired.

The hotel manager departed after he had introduced Charlotte to Captain Koroledo, and she felt a slight sense of loss at his departure. After all, his had been the only familiar face among so many unfamiliar ones, and during her two days in Suva he had endeavvoured to do his best for her.

As the ship was casting off almost immediately, she accepted the Captain's suggestion that she might retire to the cabin, and once there stretched out on the bunk in an effort to calm the uncomfortable pounding of her heart. It was all very well telling herself that Captain Koroledo was an honourable man, and that they would soon reach Manatoa; and also that she would get used to the copra-fused atmosphere, but everything had happened so swiftly,

14

and her nervous system refused to be appeased so easily.

Eventually she fumbled in her holdall and found some aspirin, and taking three with a glass of water she lay back hopefully.

The next time she opened her eyes, there was light coming through the porthole, and with a gasp she sprang off the bunk and rushed to the window. The sight that met her eyes both excited and enchanted her. They were cruising among islands, so many tiny atolls it was impossible to be sure what was real and what was reflection. Greenery gave the whole scene a backcloth, for the flamboyant colours of plants and flowers burned the senses with their beauty.

Thrusting open the port, she breathed deeply, and realized with amazement that the copra was no longer abusive to her system, in as much as it was tempered by the glorious scent of sea and vegetation.

Quickly she washed, and changed her crumpled shirt for a newly washed white one, then went up on deck. The crew eyed her curiously, but without embarrassing her, and when Captain Koroledo appeared he was still wearing his grin.

"Good morning, Miss Carlisle," he said, nodding a greeting. "Did you sleep well?"

Charlotte smiled in return. Who could be downhearted on a morning like this?

"I must have done," she exclaimed. "I don't remember much after going down to the cabin. I hope I didn't prevent you from reading your maps or anything."

The Captain shook his head. "Not at all. Actually, I must confess I sent one of my men to ask whether you required a drink before bed, but he came back with the information that you were already asleep."

Charlotte blushed scarlet. "I didn't think I would sleep. I—I was rather nervous about the trip."

"Oh?" The Captain's brows drew together. "Why?"

Charlotte sighed. "I'm afraid I'm not used to travelling so far alone."

"You are English, are you not?"

"Yes. I live in London."

"And your parents do not object to you travelling half across the world to Polynesia?" exclaimed the Captain.

"My parents are dead," replied Charlotte, sighing. "I'm an orphan. They were both on holiday in Yugoslavia several years ago, when the earthquake struck."

"I am sorry." The Captain looked genuinely concerned. "Then you are alone in the world?"

"Practically. I live with a friend. We share a flat. I have a brother, too, but he's married with a family of his own, and naturally I didn't want to interfere in their lives."

The Captain seemed surprised at this, but excusing himself went to see about some breakfast. Charlotte had a tray on her knees on a chair on deck, and enjoyed the black coffee and rolls which the galley cook provided. Afterwards she collected a book from her cabin and lay back to sunbathe, the faint breeze caused by the passage of the ship providing a pleasant airflow.

At lunch time she had shellfish and salad, and fresh fruit to follow, and then in the afternoon the ship made its first port of call. This was an island called Hanowi, and Charlotte had her first glimpse of real island life. The coming of the ship was obviously an exciting event in the lives of the islanders, and Charlotte watched from the ship's rail as Captain Koroledo went ashore and spoke to the island chief, a huge man dressed ceremoniously in a grass skirt, strings of beads about his neck.

There were children, wearing nothing at all in most cases, romping in and out of the water, splashing and screaming and having fun as any children might the world over.

Sacks of dried copra were brought aboard, and Charlotte realized that the reason she had not found the smell so distasteful this far was because of its absence, and sea air dispelling the humidity that caused the ship to temporarily shed a little of its aroma. But now it was back in full force and she retired to her cabin for a while to escape the inevitable.

The evening meal over she retired again, this time lying awake well into the night, listening to the lap-lap of the water against the sides of the vessel, and wondering with something like trepidation about the outcome of her unsolicited visit to Manatoa.

The ship reached Manatoa in the late afternoon of the following day, and anchored some distance out from the shore as there was no real harbour, and only a rowing boat or launch could negotiate the shallow waters of the island's lagoon.

It was beautiful, lying peacefully beneath a clear blue sky, but after seeing so many beautiful islands on the journey, and knowing the reason for her arrival, Charlotte could not appreciate its individuality.

Captain Koroledo joined her as she leaned on the rail, her holdall beside her.

"Well, Miss Carlisle," he said, nodding towards the luxuriant foliage that encroached almost to the water's edge, "there is Manatoa. Your destination."

"Yes." Charlotte swallowed hard. "Do you have a cargo to collect?"

"No. Manatoa is a member of an island corporation who supply their own vessels for transporting the copra back to Suva. The corporation is a large concern, owned mainly by the white planters, like Mr. Meredith, who have considerably modernized their industry by introducing their own kiln drying, and by generally clearing the undergrowth so that the fallen coconuts are easier to collect. With kiln drying the product is naturally of a higher standard."

Charlotte frowned. "I see. But I don't understand—I thought, from what the manager said, that you called regularly at Manatoa."

Captain Koroledo laughed. "Your friend from the hotel told me of your predicament. Naturally, as I pass close by Manatoa, I agreed to help you."

Charlotte bit her lip. "Oh, Captain Koroledo! What can I say? I'm very grateful to you."

"Not at all. Besides, it is possible you may have to return with me, and then I shall have the pleasure of your company for the whole trip."

Charlotte smiled. "Well, thank you, anyway."

The Captain waved her thanks away, and then looked shoreward. "Ah, we have been spotted. Look, there is someone there, on the jetty."

Sure enough Charlotte could see some children on the jetty, obviously not island children from the way they were dressed, and from the lighter cast of their skin. Then they disappeared, scampering off into the trees which successfully hid any signs of habitation from view.

A surfboat was lowered into the water, and the Captain indicated that Charlotte should climb down into it. As this meant negotiating a rope ladder, she was glad of the sturdiness of her jeans, and the firm grip provided by her sandals. The boat which rocked alarmingly as Captain Koroledo joined her was propelled enthusiastically to the jetty by one of the crew, and then Charlotte was assisted on to the stone projection.

The water in the lagoon was crystal clear, and she could see fish in their thousands, swimming and diving with effortless grace. She could also see the pearly glint of the coral bed whose sharp edges could cut one's feet to shreds.

She looked about her expectantly, able to see now that a path led through the trees towards the inner area of the island.

Captain Koroledo told his boatman to wait, and then said: "Come along, Mr. Meredith's house is not far."

As she followed Captain Koroledo through the belt of trees, that almost closed overhead, she tried to imagine a marina built on the lagoon, with a deep water harbour more fitted to sailing vessels. There would be a long low clubhouse, resembling a planter's house, she supposed, and smaller dwellings, complete in themselves for the guests. Everything would be done with the utmost taste; indeed the Hunter Agency refused to deal with companies who might attempt to deliberately commercialize unspoilt land with coarse, monolithic erections, that fought in size and purpose with the rest of the landscape.

But the proposed estate on Manatoa would enhance rather than detract from the island's natural beauty. Here would be no noisy, artificial development, but instead the kind of luxurious solitude sought by people tired of the hustle and bustle of twentieth century life. Of course, there would be entertainments of a sort, like big-game fishing or horseback riding, and maybe the atmosphere of the place could be retained by the use of native craft like palm-thatched roofs and out-rigger canoes . . .

She was so absorbed by her thoughts that Captain Koroledo had to speak twice before she realized he was addressing her.

"I'm sorry," she exclaimed. "What did you say?"

The Captain indicated ahead of them, and Charlotte caught her breath. There was the house belonging to the Merediths, the kind of low, cool building she had been visualizing for the clubhouse, with shutters at the windows, and a wide verandah, thatched with palms, and supporting comfortable, attractively-coloured garden furniture made of bamboo. There was a garden in front of the house, a veritable mass of colour, with bougainvillea and hibiscus, frangipani and flame trees, among more sedate varieties like lilies and carnations.

To the left of the house there was a kind of paddock where several cows grazed, and beyond, the jungle wove its interlacing net of creepers and shrubs.

"It's beautiful!" exclaimed Charlotte, shaking her head. "I—I must admit I didn't expect anything like this. I wonder—I wonder why . . ."

But she got no further, for two children emerged from the building, followed closely by a woman in her fifties, Charlotte estimated, who hurried towards them, looking rather hot and harassed.

"Oh, hello!" she exclaimed, with evident relief. "So you've arrived!"

Charlotte glanced at Captain Koroledo, and then frowned. "Mrs—Mrs. Meredith?" she faltered.

"Yes." The woman had reached them now, and was running a hand over her hair in an effort to reduce it to order. "I'm Mrs. Meredith." She indicated the two children who were beside her, and who Charlotte now saw were two boys, dressed similarly in shorts and T-shirts, and approximately about six and ten years old. "This is John and this is Michael."

"How do you do, John? How do you do, Michael?" said Charlotte solemnly, and then looked again at Mrs. Meredith. "Do you know Captain Koroledo?"

"Of course. Good afternoon, Captain. Thank you for your help. Will you stay and have some tea?"

But the Captain shook his head with a deprecating smile. "Unfortunately, no, Mrs. Meredith. I have not the time. This was an unscheduled call for me."

"And I'm very grateful to you," exclaimed Charlotte, still rather bewildered by so many new impressions. She turned to Mrs. Meredith. "Mr. Meredith *is* here, then?"

"Of course. He will be back very soon." Mrs. Meredith smiled. "But you must be hot and thirsty. Come along, we'll have some tea—or perhaps you would prefer something long and cool."

After bidding good-bye to the Captain, and receiving his good wishes, Charlotte followed Mrs. Meredith towards the house. The two boys, who were eyeing her rather intently, came behind, and Charlotte wondered whether Mrs. Meredith was their mother. She certainly looked older than that, but appearances could be deceptive.

Mrs. Meredith suggested that Charlotte might like to sit on the verandah for now, and later, after she had had a drink, she could see her room. Charlotte was surprised that so little concern had been shown for her abrupt arrival, and then decided that possibly distances in the islands were not considered of any importance, and as life progressed at such a leisurely pace, they probably assumed that sooner or later if Mr. Meredith didn't show up in Suva, she would show up here. It seemed an unsatisfactory arrangement but the only one she could come up with right now.

Mrs. Meredith, with that rather harassed air of someone who is coping with a situation fraught with difficulties, disappeared inside the house after she had settled Charlotte in a comfortable lounger, and the two boys lingered on the verandah steps, regarding the visitor curiously.

Charlotte smiled at them, then said: "Do you live here?"

John, who was the elder, frowned. "Of course we do," he said indifferently. "At least, we do now."

Michael moved a little closer. "Our parents are separated, you see," he confided, "so we're living here until everything is sorted out."

Charlotte was amazed at the complacency with which Michael made his statement. She sensed no apparent concern, no real sense of regret. John she was not so sure about. Being the elder he was bound to have felt the break-up of his parents' marriage more acutely.

"I'm sorry," she said inadequately, and Michael hunched his narrow shoulders.

"We're not," he said, with some arrogance. "It was all rows before!"

With some relief Mrs. Meredith came back at that moment, carrying a tray on which was a teapot and teacups, together with a jug of iced lime juice.

"Which would you prefer, Miss . . .?" Mrs. Meredith frowned. "I'm afraid I've forgotten your name."

"Carlisle," said Charlotte clearly. "Charlotte Carlisle."

"Tell me, Miss Carlisle, which would you prefer? Tea or lime?"

"Lime, please," said Charlotte, drawing out her cigarettes and offering them to Mrs. Meredith. The older woman shook her head, and pushing her hair back from her brow, heaved a sigh and sank into a chair.

"You must excuse me, Miss Carlisle, but I'm afraid I'm not used to coping with two lively children. It's some time since I had children of my own to care for, and they can be little devils, believe me! Don't let their present angelic air fool you!"

Charlotte smiled understandingly. "I'm sure you have your hands full," she agreed.

"I do have help in the house," went on Mrs. Meredith, "but Rosa, that's our maid of all work, has been taken ill, and consequently I'm finding it doubly difficult to manage. That was why I was so glad when I saw you!"

"Oh!" Charlotte digested this. She couldn't quite see how she was going to be of any assistance, unless Mrs. Meredith was talking about the planned development of Manaota. If she were then that might account for the reason that this Meredith man was selling. Now that his wife had apparently left him, this older woman must be his aunt or mother perhaps, he obviously wanted to get away as soon as possible, and Charlotte's arrival would expedite this procedure. Yes, that sounded much more reasonable.

"I must confess," went on Mrs. Meredith, "that I was expecting an older woman, from my son's description."

"Were you?" Charlotte felt as though she was speaking in monosyllables, but she couldn't help it. How could Meredith have a description of her? He had never even seen her. Then she realized; of course, Evan would have had to give him a description, so that Meredith would be able to recognize her at Nandi airport.

"Yes," went on Mrs. Meredith. "Still, never mind, it shouldn't be a long job. Just until all the details are wound up. It was lucky you were in Suva, wasn't it?"

Charlotte would scarcely have called a carefully planned trip from London to Fiji *luck*, but she managed a smile, and wished Mr. Meredith would show up.

"Is Manatoa your home?" she asked now, for something to say, more than anything.

Mrs. Meredith shook her head. "Not now, my dear. It was my home for many years, but when my husband died and my son took over the business, I decided I would like a change, too. So I moved to New Zealand. I'm very happy there. I have friends, and I play bridge, and do all the things a widow of my age usually does."

Charlotte nodded understandingly. "Do you miss—all this?"

Mrs. Meredith looked a little pensive. "Sometimes. Sometimes. I must admit that life in the islands has a charm all its own. Do you sense that, Miss Carlisle?"

Charlotte agreed vigorously. "I love it already," she replied. "There's so much luxuriance—so much colour! It's startling!"

The boys became restless and wandered away, and Mrs. Meredith rose to her feet. "Come along, my dear," she said, "I'll show you your room. My son will be back directly, and I'm sure you would like to shower and change before he arrives."

Charlotte frowned down at her jeans. Obviously Mrs. Meredith did not consider jeans suitable attire for early evening in Manatoa. What a blessing she had packed that Tricel tunic.

Her room was situated at the back of the house overlooking smooth well-kept lawns that sloped towards the impenetrable mass of the jungle. Away to the right, in the rapidly approaching gloom, Charlotte could see outbuildings and horses in another paddock. The room itself had a mosaic-tiled floor which was cool to the feet, with pink silk covers and curtains. Storm shutters and a mesh grille were at the windows, the latter, Mrs. Meredith explained, to keep out the annoying presence of night moths and other flying insects. There was an adjoining bathroom, but Mrs. Meredith regretfully explained that she must share this with the boys. After Mrs. Meredith had gone, Charlotte took out the Tricel tunic and laid it on the bed, and then collecting a change of underwear she went into the bathroom. As she switched on the electric light to alleviate the darkness she heard the whirring flutter of wings against the mesh, and felt grateful for its protection. She lingered under the shower, which was not icily cold as at the hotel, but rather lukewarm and refreshing nonetheless, then dried herself thoroughly, used talcum powder rather liberally, and dressed again.

She combed her hair into its usual knot, and applied a small amount of eye make-up and some lipstick. At last, satisfied that she was ready to meet any eventuality, she left the room and walked along the wide passage to the verandah.

The house was very quiet now, and she had thought she was alone until, as she leaned on the verandah rail enjoying the perfumes of the night air, a voice said: "Good evening, Miss Carlisle," and she almost jumped out of her skin.

She swung round, her eyes trying to probe the tropical darkness which had fallen while she took her shower, and saw a man detach himself lazily from one of the loungers and move into the light from the lantern, which was lit by the verandah door.

He was quite a tall man, with a lean muscular build. His hair appeared to be very dark, but as his face was in shadow she could not distinguish his expression. Despite the fact that she had already introduced herself to his mother she felt uncomfortably at a disadvantage.

"Mr. Meredith?" she questioned quickly.

"Yes, I'm Meredith," he replied in a quiet, attractive voice. Then he waited, as though expecting Charlotte to make some explanation for her presence here. Charlotte stumbled into words, only wanting to make her position clear, inwardly chiding herself for feeling so nervous.

"Well, thank goodness we meet at last," she said, attempting a smile. "I was beginning to think my trip was to be in vain."

"Indeed?" He inclined his head, and Charlotte

wished he would be a bit more helpful. He must know how embarrassed she was feeling.

"Yes. When you weren't at the airport to meet me, I travelled to Suva as arranged, and took a room at the hotel. I've been there two days and as you didn't contact me, naturally I was beginning to think you had had second thoughts."

The man seemed absorbed by her conversation, and moving into the light completely, he said: "I appear to have—well, caused you a great deal of trouble," he remarked lazily.

"Never mind," she said, somewhat brusquely. "I'm here now, and having seen the island, I'm sure we can do business!"

"Can we?" He smiled, revealing even white teeth. Charlotte wondered why she had the uncomfortable feeling that he was laughing *at* her. It was an unusual experience for her to feel at a disadvantage with a man, and not one which she was enjoying. Working in a job, predominantly dealing with men, she had thought she could deal with any situation. But somehow this lean, sun-tanned man, with hard, masculine features, emanated the kind of authority she had never yet had to challenge. He wasn't good-looking, and yet she was sure women would find him attractive. Was that why his wife had left him?

Trying to retain her composure, to find a point of contact, she went on: "Yes. The agency has given me permission to make a lightning assessment of the situation, and if I find everything is in order, Mr. Hunter, my employer, will arrive to act on my recommendation, to finalize the details."

The man drew out a case and extracted a cheroot which he placed between his teeth, and then lit, with deliberation. Heavens, thought Charlotte annoyedly, he was cool! He hadn't even apologized for not meeting her at Nandi!

"Could you—er—re-enlighten me about these details?" he said, studying her rather intently.

Charlotte frowned. "Surely our letters were explicit, Mr. Meredith! The Company who wish to lease this land are willing to pay a very substantial figure. Naturally we guarantee that any developments made here are to the island's advantage. The company, Belmain Estates, have various developments all over the world, and are noted for their careful consideration of natural amenities . . ."

"Belmain Estates," he murmured thoughtfully, and then Charlotte heard Mrs. Meredith's voice.

"Pat!" she was calling. "Patrick! Where are you?"

The man gave Charlotte a rueful glance, and moved to the verandah door. "I'm here, Mother," he said as Mrs. Meredith came along the passage to join them.

Charlotte pressed a bewildered hand to her throat, and as he turned back to her, he said:

"Yes, Miss Carlisle; in answer to your unspoken question, I am Patrick Meredith! The man I believe you expected to meet was my cousin, Andrew Meredith!"

Charlotte stared at him. "I see! Oh, what a fool you must think me! No wonder you were unaware of the details. Does—does your cousin own land on the island, too?"

Patrick Meredith straightened, and for a moment his expression was harsh. "My cousin owns a strip of land on the far side of the island," he replied bleakly. "I myself have been endeavouring to buy that piece of land for the past ten years! Unfortunately, he refuses to sell to me. However, until your arrival, I was in ignorance of his proposed plans for it, so for this information I'm grateful!"

Charlotte was horrified. "You mean—you let me tell you all about it, knowing I was betraying a confidence!" she gasped.

Patrick Meredith frowned. "I'm sorry, Miss Carlisle, for using you in this way, but when it concerns Manatoa, I would use any means in my power to prevent the kind of development you have outlined to me!"

CHAPTER TWO

MRS, MEREDITH, stared with some confusion at her son.

"But, Patrick," she explained, "I thought Miss Carlisle was the young woman you had engaged in Suva to take care of John and Michael!"

Patrick Meredith lifted his broad shoulders indifferently. "I'm sorry, Mother, I've never seen this young woman before in my life!"

Now Mrs. Meredith turned to Charlotte, her eyes rather impatient. "But, Miss Carlisle, you let me believe you'd come to help us . . ."

Charlotte had never felt so embarrassed, and she was quite sure that Patrick Meredith was aware of it. It was infuriating, doubly so when she imagined what Evan would say when he discovered what she had done. And there was still Andrew Meredith!

Swallowing hard, she said: "I'm afraid you and I were talking at cross purposes, Mrs. Meredith."

Mrs. Meredith shook her head. Then she looked at her son again. "Well, what does this young woman want? If she hasn't come to help us, why is she here? I certainly didn't employ her, and if you didn't——"

"Calm down!" Patrick Meredith was beginning to look slightly amused at the situation. "Why don't you ask Miss Carlisle why she's here?"

Charlotte glared at him. "That won't be necessary!" She clenched her fists and said: "I came, Mrs. Meredith, because I had an arrangement—a business arrangement—to meet Mr. Meredith, Mr. *Andrew* Meredith, that is, in Nandi, five days ago. When he didn't show up, neither there nor at the hotel in Suva, I found that I could take the copra boat to Manatoa, so that's what I did." She sighed. When I arrived, I had no reason to suspect that you were not related to Andrew Meredith, had I?"

"That sounds plausible, Mother," remarked Patrick easily, and Charlotte gave him another angry glance.

"It's not only plausible, Mr. Meredith, it's the truth," she exclaimed hotly. Although it was considerably cooler now than it had been in the heat of the day, it was still very warm, and Charlotte was aware that this altercation was causing the palms of her hands to moisten uncomfortably.

Patrick Meredith shrugged. "I'm sure it is." He drew on his cheroot. "Andrew is planning to lease Coralido to Belmain Estates, a development corporation!"

Mrs. Meredith gasped, and Charlotte felt terrible. It was bad enough knowing she had made an absolute mess of the job she had been sent to do without experiencing Mrs. Meredith's appalled reaction to the scheme. Linking her fingers together, she said, as coolly as possible: "Perhaps, as Mr. Meredith lives on the far side of the island, you could direct me to his house."

Patrick Meredith leant back against one of the posts of the verandah, while Mrs. Meredith sank down on to a chair, obviously still shocked at her son's revelation.

"I could, although I doubt whether it would do you any good. He isn't there. He left Manatoa several days ago."

Charlotte felt that this was the last straw. Not only had she journeyed all this way in vain, but now probably Andrew Meredith would be hanging around Suva, waiting for her. Quelling the angry exclamation that sprang to her lips, she said bleakly: "Then perhaps you could tell me how I can get back to Suva!"

"You can't!" Patrick Meredith was openly grinning now, a kind of malicious enjoyment in his expression. "At least not for another month or so. Few trading boats call at Manatoa, and Andrew left on the last one. There won't be another for quite some time."

Charlotte compressed her lips. Of course, that would amuse Patrick Meredith. The longer he kept her and his cousin apart, the greater were the chances of the deal not going through.

Mrs. Meredith eyed her son strangely, opened her mouth as though to say something, and then closed it again.

Charlotte moved restlessly. "But I can't stay here for a week, let alone a month!" she cried. "I have a job to do!"

"I'm afraid your job will have to wait," remarked Patrick Meredith coolly. "After all, you can hardly blame us for your inefficiency. Surely this agency you say you work for has more businesslike representatives!"

Charlotte stiffened. "I'm perfectly capable of conducting my business in the normal way," she said. "Obviously, had Mrs. Meredith revealed more explicity who she was expecting I would not have troubled either her or you, and I could have returned with the Captain on the copra ship!"

Mrs. Meredith looked up. "You had plenty of opportunity to state your business," she said, rather shortly, and Charlotte flushed.

Patrick Meredith stubbed out his cheroot. "Let's not make this situation any more ridiculous by arguing about it!" he said abruptly. "Is dinner ready?" and at his mother's nod, "Then I suggest we eat and discuss this later."

The meal, a delicious concoction of shellfish and rice, followed by fruit and coffee, might have been sawdust for all the enjoyment Charlotte derived from it. It was as well that the boys joined them, for their inconsequential chatter disguised the fact of Charlotte's preoccupation. Her mind buzzed dizzily with the complications she had created for herself, and she silently cursed her own impatience that had persuaded her to make this journey in the first place. Right now she could have been dining in the hotel in Suva, and sooner or later Andrew Meredith would be bound to appear.

Pushing aside her plate, she stared moodily about the room. Even so, she had to appreciate the charm of its decoration, a gentle blend of blues and greens and lemons creating a cool, restful appearance. Tall lamps provided electric lighting, and she presumed the island must have its own generator. It seemed ridiculous that such civilized accommodation could exist on an island so cut off from civilization.

Making an effort to be sociable, she said: "Tell me, Mr. Meredith, are you the only white planter on the island?"

Patrick Meredith finished his meal and lit a cheroot before replying. Then, when his mother went for the coffee, he said:

"I own most of the island, Miss Carlisle. The only stretch I do not own is owned by my cousin, Andrew Meredith. However, as the island is only part of a combine of islands whose owners have joined together in an effort to create a copra corporation with its own shipping methods and so on, I employ several white men, as well as Indians and Melanesians."

"Oh." Charlotte digested this. "Then there are other white families on the island?"

"There are five other white families on the island, yes," replied Patrick Meredith slowly. "Do you mind telling me why you're so interested in our set-up here? Is this more information for your agency?"

Charlotte gritted her teeth. "Not at all, Mr. Meredith. It merely occurred to me that maybe someone else might be able to offer a suggestion as to how I could leave the island?"

Patrick rose from the table. "My dear Miss Carlisle, my employees are not here for your convenience. I've told you that the trading vessel calls only rarely."

Charlotte rose too, aware that the two boys were becoming intensely interested in their exchange. "Mr. Meredith, you don't seem to understand, I *have* to get back to Suva! I'm here in Fiji solely for the purpose of incorporating this deal! My employer, Evan Hunter, of the Hunter Agency, will require reports from me. What do you think he'll imagine has happened to me if I disappear for months?" She ended on a high note, conscious of a rising sense of hysteria at the hopelessness of her situation.

Patrick moved out of the dining-room on to the verandah, and said: "Come and sit down, Miss Carlisle. There is no point in exciting yourself unnecessarily. I realize how you feel, believe me. But even you must be able to see that I'm as helpless to help you as you are yourself. My only suggestion is that as you've come here to see my cousin, it's logical

34

that when he arrives in Suva and discovers you've left for Manatoa, he may return here immediately to meet you."

Charlotte heaved a sigh, and seated herself in one of the loungers with a sense of finality. Accepting a cigarette which he offered her from a box on the glass-topped table, she drew on it gratefully. After all, as Patrick Meredith had said, it was no use railing against a fate which was implacable anyway. She would just have to do as he said, and wait, and hope that Andrew Meredith would discover her where-abouts soon.

Mrs. Meredith returned with the tray of coffee. "I've just seen Rosa," she said to Patrick with some relief. "She's much better, and she expects to be back tomorrow, thank goodness!" She seated herself opposite Charlotte. "Coffee, Miss Carlisle?"

"Yes, thank you." Charlotte leaned forward to accept a cup, and Mrs. Meredith studied her with some concern.

"Are you feeling quite well, Miss Carlisle? You look rather pale, and I noticed that you ate very little at dinner. Was it not to your liking?"

Charlotte shook her head. "The meal was delicious," she said hastily. "But I'm afraid I wasn't very hungry."

"Miss Carlisle is finding it difficult to accept the remoteness of our life here," remarked Patrick, watching his mother rather closely, Charlotte thought.

Mrs. Meredith made no reply, but merely smoothed the pleats of her skirt rather nervously.

Charlotte looked at her host. "If what you say is true, then I have no alternative but to ask you to

35

allow me to stay—at least, until Andrew Meredith comes back."

Patrick shrugged. "Naturally you will stay here." He lit a cheroot. "My mother, for one, will be glad of your company."

Charlotte doubted that this was true. Mrs. Meredith already seemed to have her hands full.

"Possibly Miss Carlisle could help to keep John and Michael out of mischief," said Mrs. Meredith, sipping her coffee. "There are too many places here where they could injure themselves!"

"Oh, really, Mother," exclaimed Patrick impatiently. "They're not made of glass! Jennifer had no scruples about leaving them!"

Charlotte replaced her coffee cup on the tray, and refused Mrs. Meredith's offer of a second cup. "Oh, really," she said, glancing back at the boys who had finished their meal and were again listening to the adults' conversation. "I'm quite prepared to do anything I can to help. It's the least I can do," although as she said this, Charlotte remembered the shameless way Patrick Meredith had allowed her to reveal all her plans to him, knowing full well that she was unaware of his identity, and pressed the palms of her hands together to alleviate the sense of frustration that enveloped her.

Already, here, drinking coffee on the verandah, she was allowing the warmth and peace of the night to lull her into a false state of security. Never for a moment must she allow her surroundings to influence her, for obviously, just as Patrick Meredith had felt great satisfaction at the frustration of her plans, he would take every opportunity to attempt to deflect her from her ultimate goal.

Mrs. Meredith seemed to sense Charlotte's misgivings, for she said quickly:

"Miss Carlisle has had a long day, Patrick. Perhaps it would be a good idea if she went to bed now. I'm sure she's longing to relax completely."

Charlotte seized this suggestion gratefully. After all, tomorrow was another day, and maybe some unforeseen happening might bring a trading vessel to the island, and enable her return to Suva at once.

Charlotte didn't think she would sleep, in fact she was sure she wouldn't. But the softness of the bed, after the rather hard bunk in Captain Koroledo's cabin, was soothing and relaxing, and even the sounds of the night animals in the jungle only a few feet away from her bedroom window did not trouble her.

Thoughts troubled her for a while. So many things had happened since she left England and it was difficult to assimilate them with any degree of clarity. What would Evan think of all this? However could she justify herself to him? After all, he was expecting to join her quite soon, and if Andrew Meredith did not find that she had left for Manatoa heaven knew what construction Evan might place on her disappearance.

Then she scoffed the thought aside. One or both of them was bound to find that she had sailed on the *Fijian Star*. The hotel manager knew and he was a gregarious person, perfectly capable of volunteering the information even without being asked.

She rolled on to her stomach. The other thing on her mind was her careless revelations of Andrew Meredith's plans to his cousin. She supposed that ought not to have been a problem, but it was obvious from Patrick Meredith's attitude that they were antagonistic towards one another. But anyway, she argued, there was nothing Patrick Meredith could actually do to prevent Andrew Meredith from leasing them his land, was there?

She punched her pillow into shape. It was no use worrying. For good or ill, she was here in Patrick Meredith's house, and that was the end of it. Unbidden came thoughts of John and Michael and their rather adult attitude to their parents' proposed separation. It seemed terrible that they should have to face the inevitable conflict that arose between children and individual parents. Why had Patrick Meredith's wife left him at all? Had the isolation been too much for her? Had she desired the bright lights of city life? Or had they merely been incompatible? It was difficult to decide, not knowing either his wife or their circumstances, and she didn't really know why the thoughts plagued her mind, but they did. Maybe it was the realization that living for some time in close proximity with a man like Patrick Meredith could be dangerous.

When next she opened her eyes, the sun was filtering through the shutters on her windows, allowing brilliant slashes of colour to probe at her eyes. She lay still for a moment, unable to remember where she was, and then, as consciousness returned fully, it all came back to her: Manatoa, Mrs. Meredith, John and Michael, and their father, Patrick Meredith.

With an abrupt movement she slid out of bed, and crossing the floor which was pleasantly cool to her bare feet, she threw wide the shutters.

The previous afternoon and evening there had been so many other matters to concern herself with that she had not taken a great deal of notice of the garden at the back of the house, but now she could see that someone had taken great pains to create an oasis of order and serenity at the edge of the wild abandon of the jungle. Even so, she realized how difficult it must be to retain any kind of order here, where flowers grew to fullness in one day and died the same night. Weeds were a constant menace, and like everything else here, grew in profusion.

Leaving the window, she walked to the bathroom door, opening it thoughtlessly, and coming upon John,

"Oh, I'm sorry," she said, smiling at him, not feeling at all embarrassed despite the fact that she was only wearing a pair of shortie pyjamas. She liked John, and thought that she could make a friend of him. His younger brother was, as yet, untroubled by life and its problems, but Charlotte felt that John's attempts at adult speech were the outcome of his parents' lack of relationship. He was trying to grow up overnight, and that was bad.

Now John said: "Gran said we should use the bathroom early so as to leave it free for you. Mike's already finished. He isn't very thorough, I'm afraid."

Charlotte leant against the door. "And you are, I suppose," she smiled.

John rinsed his mouth and shrugged. He was very serious. "If you don't keep your teeth clean, they go bad," he said, drying his face. "That's right, isn't it?"

Charlotte nodded. "Of course. But sometimes, if there's something one particularly wants to do, one can forget."

"Do you forget?"

"Not often."

"My dad—" he faltered, then went on: "—my dad always used to say that teeth were the most important part of a person's appearance."

Charlotte frowned. "He *used* to say that. Doesn't he say it now?"

John's expression became withdrawn. "I don't know what he says now," he said enigmatically, and went out of the bathroom, through the door into his own bedroom.

Charlotte frowned, and then shrugging perplexedly, she walked across and pushed the bolt into position. Then, stripping off her pyjamas, she took a quick shower. As she cleaned her own teeth, she pondered John's strange statement. Obviously, John blamed his father for the break-up of the marriage, at least that was the only logical explanation Charlotte could come up with.

She looked at her holdall rather regretfully, as she put on slim-fitting cotton pants and a sleeveless Italian printed overblouse. She had brought three pairs of pants and several blouses, but only the one dress, so Mrs. Meredith would have to get used to seeing her about in trousers, unless there was a store on the island, which seemed the height of improbability.

Emerging from her room, she walked along the passage to the verandah where Mrs. Meredith had told her they usually ate during the hours of daylight. It was still quite early, barely eight o'clock, and she wondered whether Mrs. Meredith or Rosa, the housemaid, was about. To her surprise, she found not Mrs. Meredith on the verandah, drinking coffee and smoking a cigarette, but a girl of about her own age, with hair as dark as hers was fair, long and smooth, and loose about her shoulders. Dressed in short pink shorts and a halter-necked top of white cotton, she looked cool and very attractive.

She glanced up as Charlotte appeared, and gave her an appraising look, before she ventured a small smile. "Hello," she said, her accent most definitely French. "You must be Miss Carlisle. How do you do? I am Yvonne Dupré."

Charlotte smiled in return, and at Yvonne Dupré's waved invitation, seated herself opposite her. "How do you do?" she said, rather nervously. And then: "Thank you," when Yvonne poured her a cup of coffee and pushed it towards her. "Do you live on the island, Miss Dupré?"

The girl nodded. *"Oui.* My father is a scientist. He works here on Manatoa. First and foremost he is a doctor, and as Patrick employs in the region of two hundred men, there are many things to keep him busy. The men have wives and families to care for, and in his spare time my father studies tropical medicine. This is his real love."

"I see," Charlotte nodded. "And have you lived here all your life, Miss Dupré?"

"Oh, no, Miss Carlisle. I was born in Paris. My father has only lived here for the past five years. To begin with I was still at school, a finishing school, you understand, but afterwards I came back to live here, to care for him. My mother is dead. She died before we left Paris."

Charlotte gave a sympathetic smile. "And you like it, I gather." She flushed. "Living here, I mean."

41

"Oh, but of course. I adore the islands. I am an outdoor girl, Miss Carlisle. I adore all water sports water-skiing, skin-diving, sailing, or just swimming. And besides, Manatoa is my home."

Charlotte sipped her coffee, wondering how much Yvonne Dupré knew of her reasons for being here. Obviously, at some time between last night and this morning, she had been informed of her arrival. Maybe she knew Andrew Meredith, too.

"Tell me," said Charlotte, "do you know Andrew Meredith?"

"Of course. I know everybody on the island." She wrinkled her small nose. "That is not to say I like them all!"

Charlotte contained her impatience. "I—well, I gather there's no love lost between Andrew Meredith and his cousin."

"*No love lost.* What is that?" questioned Yvonne curiously.

"She means we don't like one another," remarked a voice which had startled Charlotte once before.

She swung round, to find Patrick Meredith mounting the verandah steps. He had apparently been swimming, for his hair was wet, and the shorts he was wearing were damp from his body. Charlotte turned round again, concentrating on her coffee, while Yvonne's features curved into a welcoming smile.

"Darling," she exclaimed, "I was beginning to think you had drowned!" She caught his head, and raised it to her lips in a gesture that from an English-woman would have looked affected. "Miss Carlisle and I have been getting to know one another."

Charlotte averted her eyes from this little display. It was all very well being affectionate, but Patrick

Meredith was still a married man, even if his wife had left him. And if this was the way Yvonne thought about him, then perhaps she had had reasons for leaving. As for the boys. . . .

Patrick released himself from Yvonne's clinging fingers and flung himself lazily into a chair beside Charlotte.

"Well, Miss Carlisle," he said lazily, "did you sleep well?"

"Very well, thank you Mr. Meredith," replied Charlotte, managing to sound cool and slightly disparaging.

Patrick grinned. "Yvonne, I don't think our Miss Carlisle approves of our behaviour."

Charlotte's cheeks burned anew. "Mr. Meredith, what you and Miss Dupré choose to do is no concern of mine."

"No, it's not. Yet I sense a certain—how shall I put it—disapproving note in your voice. I wonder why?"

Yvonne frowned. "Stop teasing Miss Carlisle, Patrick. Is it not frustrating enough for her to find herself stranded here, without you making fun of her too?"

Patrick sighed. "Pour me some coffee, love, and then I must go down to the kilns. I promised Macmaster I would see him this morning."

"But you promised to take me sailing!" wailed Yvonne.

"Not today, Yvonne, sorry. There's too much to do."

"Oh, Patrick!" Yvonne made a *move* with her lips, pouting prettily, and then Michael came bounding along the verandah from his room, almost sprawling all over the table as he tripped over his feet. "Michael!" exclaimed Yvonne, forgetting herself for a moment. "Do be careful!"

Michael made a face at her, and then gave Patrick Meredith a cheeky grin. "Can I come with you to the kilns, Uncle Patrick?" he asked appealingly.

Charlotte stared at him, then transferred her gaze to his uncle, Patrick Meredith, as though aware of her scrutiny, glanced at her.

"I gather you thought John and Michael were mine," he remarked lazily.

Charlotte lifted her shoulders. "It was a natural assumption."

"Haven't you learned to be wary of them yet?" he parried, and she knew to what he was referring.

"Obviously not," she said, looking down at her fingers.

Patrick caught Michael between his knees. "Yes," he said, "you can come with me. But not if you persist in treating Yvonne to this rudeness! Now say you're sorry for making a face at her!"

"Must I?" Michael grimaced.

"Michael!" said his uncle warningly.

"Oh, all right," said Michael with ill-grace. "Sorry, Yvonne."

Yvonne wrinkled her nose. It was obviously a habit with her. "You are a naughty boy, Michael, for I know you do not mean it."

"Oh, stuff!" said Michael, under his breath.

"What did you say?" exclaimed Patrick, as he wriggled, trying to get away.

Charlotte hid a smile. There was something endaring about Michael, for all his cheekiness. She wanted to laugh, to relieve some of the tension she had been feeling. Patrick Meredith was right, she jumped to conclusions too easily. She would have to stop and think in future.

Mrs. Meredith appeared just then, accompanied by a dark-skinned Fijian girl, whom she introduced to Charlotte as Rosa.

"You haven't eaten yet, Miss Carlisle," she exclaimed. "Pat and Yvonne had breakfast hours ago. We all rise early round here."

Immediately Charlotte felt that rising at eight o'clock was the middle of the morning.

"I'm afraid I overslept then," she excused herself.

"Nonsense," retorted Patrick, looking challengingly at his mother. "Heavens, civilized people don't get up in the middle of the night, as we do."

Mrs. Meredith patted his shoulder impatiently "For goodness' sake, Patrick, if you're going to the kilns, go! You delight in causing trouble. I'm quite sure Miss Carlisle and I can work out a suitable timetable."

"She's not here for your benefit," replied Patrick, rising to his feet. He looked at Charlotte. "Or for mine either," he added mockingly. "Cousin Andrew is the lucky man! I wonder if he's cognizant of that fact?"

"Will you stop tormenting the child, and go!" exclaimed his mother again. "Rosa, see what Miss Carlisle usually has for breakfast while I deal with Patrick and the boys'.

"The boys can come with me," said Patrick easily, lighting one of the cheroots which Charlotte had seen him smoking the previous day. "That will give you all time to get used to one another."

He walked to the verandah steps, and Yvonne slipped off her chair to link her arm with his. "Oh, Mr. Meredith!" Charlotte halted their progress, and

Yvonne looked round rather impatiently herself now.

"Yes?" Patrick stopped, one foot raised to the low wall of the verandah.

"There isn't—I mean, there really is no way I can contact Suva?"

Rosa said: "Oh, but—" and Mrs. Meredith interrupted her.

"No," she answered Charlotte's question herself. "No way at all!"

Rosa looked puzzled, and Charlotte felt the faintest twinges of apprehension. They couldn't possibly be hiding anything from her, could they? She swallowed hard and said: "If—if there is a way, I should advise you to tell me—now."

Her words fell into the gentle warmth of the morning air, and for a moment there was complete silence. And then Patrick Meredith moved. He straightened to his full height and said:

"Are you threatening me, Miss Carlisle?"

"Threatening you? No, of course not. It just occurs to me that you might not be telling me the whole truth. After all, it's in your interest to prevent this deal going through. You said so yourself." Charlotte was annoyed to find her voice trembling over the last couple of words.

"Yes, I did say that. And I meant it. And, as you say, if there is some way of getting off the island, I should be most unlikely to tell you."

He turned and without saying another word, walked away.

Charlotte found herself trembling all over. This was a situation she had never even dreamed of facing. And of course she might be jumping to needless conclusions again, imagining things that simply were not possible. Surely, among all these

46

people, they could not hope to keep her a prisoner? No, that was just stupid!

Nevertheless, she was virtually just that, and as Patrick Meredith was so obviously aware, there was absolutely nothing she could do about it.

CHAPTER THREE

AFTER PATRICK MEREDITH and the two boys had departed, accompanied by a sulky Yvonne, Charlotte had her breakfast. She refused the offer of hot rolls, and accepted fruit instead, and more coffee. Mrs. Meredith disappeared for a while, obviously involved with Rosa and household chores, then reappeared and joined Charlotte at the table.

"I think perhaps it would be a good idea if I gave you an idea of the general layout here," she said thoughtfully. "After all, if you are staying for any length of time, you will soon grow tired of the gardens here, and you'll want to go bathing, I suppose."

Charlotte lit a cigarette. "Yes," she said awkwardly, conscious of the older woman's reserve. Then, attempting to act naturally, she went on: "Is there—well, perhaps somewhere that I could buy a couple of dresses? You see, I've only brought one, as I didn't expect to be staying . . ." Again that awful topic. There seemed no avoiding it.

Mrs. Meredith bit her lip. "I'm afraid we don't have any stores on Manatoa. However, one can purchase material from the trading vessels, and as I have several lengths lying waiting being made up, I could probably let you have some."

Charlotte traced the pattern of the bamboo on her chair arm. "Thank you," she said, wondering how to explain that she had never made herself a dress in her life. She looked up. "I'm afraid I'm not a very expert seamstress, Mrs. Meredith."

Mrs. Meredith's expression relaxed a little. "My dear girl, I'm not suggesting you should make up the material yourself. Rosa is a wonderful tailoress. She makes clothes for several women on Manatoa."

Charlotte sighed. "Oh, I see," she said, with some relief. "Then of course I'd be very grateful if she could help me."

Mrs. Meredith nodded, and then, with emphasis, she said: "I must confess, now that I know why you're here, I find it extremely difficult to keep my feelings to myself!"

Charlotte drew on her cigarette. "Oh? Why?"

The older woman shrugged. "Well, you must be aware of the incongruity of your position, Miss Carlisle. That we should be entertaining someone whose sole reason for being here is to disrupt the life of Manatoa is absolutely infuriating! Surely you can understand that?"

Charlotte rested her elbows on the table. "I hear what you say, Mrs. Meredith, but I can't honestly understand your attitude. Heavens! The development planned for Manatoa isn't some frivolous holiday camp. It's a perfectly sound business venture, planned to provide accommodation for a few—and I mean a few—possibly retired or quiet-living couples, who want something different from the usual run-of-the-mill resorts. We're not going to open a gambling casino, or a bingo hall, or anything monstrously out of place on an island like this!"

Mrs. Meredith gave a derisive sniff. "Miss Carlisle, the Meredith family has owned this island for many, many years. It has never been divided as it is now."

"But why is it divided?" asked Charlotte.

"I'll explain if you're really interested." Charlotte nodded, and she continued: "My husband's father, Patrick's and Andrew's grandfather, owned the whole of Manatoa. But he had two sons, and of course, when he died the island was left equally to John and Gordon. Gordon was Andrew's father. But what he couldn't have foreseen was that after his premature death—he was killed during the war—Gordon just up and left Manatoa."

Charlotte frowned. "Leaving John to take care of the plantation?"

"That's right. John, of course, was Patrick's father. But both Patrick and Andrew were young children in those days. Andrew's mother and I were friends. She was heartbroken when Gordon left Manatoa, and she died soon after in New Zealand."

"I suppose your husband's brother still owned half of the island, though," said Charlotte, frowning.

"Oh, yes, but not for long. After Margaret's death, Gordon soon ran into debt. He had a job—he worked for some engineering company, I believe, but his salary was never adequate for his needs, and gradually, over a period of years, he got into serious difficulties. We weren't well off ourselves in those days, but Gordon persuaded John to settle his debts in return for some of his land." Mrs. Meredith sighed. "Of course, John was a sentimental fool. Gordon really had little right to claim any share in the island's profits, when he refused to do anything towards its upkeep, but I think John thought that eventually he would own the whole island again, as his father had done. After all, Gordon wasn't cut out for this kind of life, and sooner or later he was bound to sell out completely."

"I see," Charlotte nodded, beginning to see a little of the pattern. "What happened?"

"Well, Gordon's rate of living was bad for his heart, and he died, quite young. Andrew was still at school, and John continued to pay his school fees. It wasn't until afterwards, when Andrew came back to Manatoa, that we discovered the hatred he held for us. Maybe Gordon had bred these thoughts in his mind, I don't know. I only know that Andrew had no intention of allowing John to buy the land, Coralido, as it's called, and what was more he built a fence around it, around the house that had once been his mother and father's home and is now little more than a ruin, and then went back to New Zealand. From time to time he comes and stays for a while, but we seldom see him. But the island is small, and such news travels."

Charlotte shook her head. "And when did he first come back?"

"Oh, about ten years ago. My husband died, knowing that the island was still divided. Patrick took over, and naturally resentment has hardened." She pushed back her chair impatiently, and stood up. "We've tried to buy that land numerous times— we've offered Andrew far above its market value, but he was simply not interested. He was prepared to wait for a more subtle chance to have his revenge. Your agency has supplied him with that chance!"

Charlotte stubbed out her cigarette, her brain a mass of conflicting emotions. Of course Mrs. Meredith's story was biased. Of course she was merely stating her side of the case, and yet it was impossible not to sympathize with the hopelessness of their position. Maybe if she had known all the facts before she left England, she would not have con-

templated dealing with such a complex situation'
She wondered if Evan had known. It seemed possible'
Evan was first and foremost a businessman, and he
would harbour no emotional thoughts on the problems of the Meredith family. Coralido was not an
emotional issue. It was just another deal, and it was
only because she was a woman that she was allowing
emotion to enter into it. She felt impatient with herself. She had always prided herself on her cool,
logical brain, and she must accept, right now, that
Mrs. Meredith's reasons for revealing these personal
matters was motivated not from any desire to
confide, but rather in an effort to involve Charlotte
emotionally.

Hardening her heart, she said: "I'm sorry, Mrs.
Meredith, believe me! I can see your difficulties, but
you must understand that I'm not the arbiter of your
fate. If Andrew Meredith chooses to lease Coralido
to Belmain Estates, then we're simply the—how shall
I put it?—*entrepreneurs*! If we didn't take up the
option, believe me, someone else would, and possibly
someone with less integrity than Belmain Estates!"

Mrs. Meredith moved to the verandah rail,
gripping the wood so hard that the knuckles of her
hands turned white.

"Believe me, Miss Carlisle," she said, in a tight
voice, "you have absolutely no notion of the ferment
your arrival has created! That Manatoa, this island
that my husband tried hard to develop for the
corporation, should be threatened by a tourist
colony, no matter how select, horrifies me!"

Charlotte sighed, standing up too. "Oh, Mrs.
Meredith," she murmured gently, "try and understand my position, too. I have a job to do. Can't we
forget about this for now? There's nothing either of

us can actually do about it anyway." She ran her tongue over her dry lips. "Perhaps you might show me a little of the island, if you wouldn't mind, of course."

Mrs. Meredith's expression was bitter. "With a view to further development?" she asked harshly. "No, thank you! If you want to explore Manatoa, Miss Carlisle, then you will have to do so alone!"

Charlotte walked thoughtfully through the belt of trees to the beach, the way she had arrived with Captain Koroledo the previous day. She had had such high hopes when she arrived at Manatoa, imagining the proposed development with confident speculation.

Now, in the course of twenty-four hours, so many things had happened to change her mind, and although she would do her utmost to agree to Andrew Meredith's terms, she had not the enthusiasm that had previously enveloped her.

Reaching the small jetty, she walked along it, idly staring out to sea. In the distance, she could see the outline of another island, but from its height and craggy appearance she realized it must be one of the atolls that abounded in these seas, little more than sand and rock, legendary coral isles.

Trudging her feet, she turned and walked back to the beach. She half-wished she had brought her swim-suit. The waters of the lagoon were clear, and only now could she see the reef that formed a natural barrier to the harbouring of larger vessels. Yesterday, she and Captain Koroledo had arrived in the surf-boat, so there must be a small inlet, big enough for that kind of craft. She wondered how many boats called at the island in a year. It seemed incredible that the service should be so poor. Of course, the island was almost self-sufficient. There were all the usual domestic animals near to the Meredith's bungalow, and crops grew to fruition readily enough.

Looking along the beach, she discovered a natural pathway leading towards the headland, and shading her eyes she could see that the inner geography of the island rose steeply to thickly clad hills that could be seen above the disguising belt of jungle. Of course, it must be quite a large island, she supposed, with the copra plantation and the necessary homes for its workers, and curiosity became uppermost in her mind. When Patrick Meredith had departed for the kilns, she had heard the sound of a vehicle, possibly a Land Rover, so apparently to explore the whole of the island, she would require transport.

Still, for all the heat of the sun it was still morning, and not oppressive yet, and she began to walk along the path towards the headland. She slid the dark glasses back on to her nose, and brought out the crumpled packet of cigarettes. She discovered she had very few left, and wondered if she could buy them here. Surely the Merediths must keep a supply.

She met no one on her walk, and it was getting quite late when she reached the foot of a small chasm, down which tumbled a clear waterfall. It was very pretty, the cleft lined with flowers of every description. She supposed it would be possible to climb to the headland from here, but as it was nearing lunch time, and she was growing rather tired, that adventure would have to wait for another day. The ferns were beautiful though, and she couldn't resist gathering an armful to take back to the bungalow. Their delicate fronds would enhance the more exotic blooms of the flowers.

It was as she was gathering the ferns that she felt something crawling up her arm. With the instinctive recoil of the female towards the insect, she jerked her head to see a spider about the size of a small coin halted there, obviously startled by her nervousness.

"Oh, God!" she breathed, a natural horror of spiders heightened by the knowledge that there were poisonous insects here as well as innocuous ones.

She didn't know what to do, whether to brush it off, or to stay perfectly still and hope it would go, and quickly. She tried to do the latter, but her senses were too acute, and with a gasp she tried to sweep it off. As she did so, she felt a slight pain, and as it fell into the ferns that she had dropped about her feet, she saw the bite on her arm.

She couldn't believe it. It had happened so quickly. And yet there was the proof, and her heart pounded suffocatingly, her throat drying up so that she felt as though she was choking.

"Calm yourself, Charlotte!" she told herself insistently, as panic rose inside her. "Don't panic! Use your head!"

Even so, she moved swiftly to separate the clinging fronds of the ferns from her feet, stepping back on to the damp sand, only to feel yet another movement beneath her feet this time.

It was a sand crab, disturbed from its sleep by the pressure of her feet. It scuttled away with its curious side-like movements towards a pile of broken coconut shells that lay about the beach beneath the palms that fringed its edging, burrowing back into the sand as fast as it could.

Charlotte shivered, and although the day was hot she felt chilled. With legs like jelly, and the certain knowledge growing inside her that she was about to die a horrible death, she turned and began to run towards the jetty and the Merediths' house beyond. What had seemed like a comfortable walk earlier had now assumed the proportions of a marathon, and the pain in her arm seemed to be intensifying, slowing her steps to a stumbling trot. She was sweating profusely, and her hair, so smooth and soft earlier, seemed lank and lifeless, damp about her shoulders. Her breath began to come in a series of sobbing gasps, and the pounding of her heart was like an actual throbbing beat in her ears.

She had reached the jetty, and was leaning gasping against a tree, trying to get her breath back, when she heard the sound of voices, and jerking up her head she saw Patrick Meredith coming along the path between the trees, accompanied by John and Michael. He had been amusing them with some story, for the boys were giggling helplessly, completely without the unnatural hauteur that had previously surrounded them.

When Patrick saw her he quickened his step, saying something to the boys so that they fell back, waiting for their uncle to reach Charlotte. Patrick faced her, an impatient expression in his eyes.

"Haven't you got any more sense than to run in this heat?" he exclaimed, grasping her shoulders and drawing her up away from the tree. He saw her burning cheeks, and the terrified expression in her eyes, and frowned: "In God's name, what's happened? Has someone molested you?

Charlotte shook her head, groping for words. "No—that is—look! I've been bitten! By a spider!"

She held out her arm, and he released her shoulders, to grip her arm tightly, pressing his fingers against the reddened flesh where the insect had

bitten her. Then he dropped her arm and shook
his head.

"Is this the cool, collected Miss Carlisle I see
before me?" His tone was amused now, and Charlotte looked down at her arm, and rubbed it vigorously.

"Don't—don't be so sarcastic!" she cried. "Is—
is it—is it poisonous?" Her voice faltered.

Patrick Meredith cupped his chin with one hand.
"Well—" he said, slowly and deliberately, "On a
lightning diagnosis, I would say that definitely—oh,
yes, definitely, there's every likelihood of—well—"

"Oh, stop it!" she exclaimed bitterly. "You're
deliberately trying to frighten me!"

"Why? What have I said?" He stood with his
hands on his hips, grinning at her, and for all her
earlier fears she was intensely conscious of the lean
muscular suppleness of his body, and the dark
attraction of eyes that held nothing but amusement.

"You're deliberately tormenting me!" she accused him.

Patrick turned away, glancing at John and
Michael. "Am I doing that?" he asked innocently.
"It seems, boys, that we have a very severe case
here. An urgent case of arachnaphobia!"

Charlotte's brain wouldn't function. "What's
that?" she gasped.

Patrick laughed. "Simply—fear of spiders!" he
said.

Charlotte compressed her lips. "Oh! You—
you're hateful!" she exclaimed angrily. "How you
must be enjoying this!"

Patrick shrugged. "Well, I must confess I am
amazed that the cool business woman of yesterday

57

should disintegrate so completely over such a small thing!"

Charlotte drew herself up to her full height, unwillingly aware that at his words some of the pain had left her arm. She was not an hysteric, but surely anyone would have reacted as she had done!

"I did not disintegrate," she said now, looking down at her arm. "Heavens! How was I supposed to know whether the spider was poisonous or not? Anyone in my position would have panicked—"

"Not necessarily," he interrupted her. "A man would have reasoned that where there's a poison there is also an antidote!"

"Oh, you're so blasted clever, aren't you?" she cried, brushing back her hair with a careless hand. "I wish I'd never come here!"

"Believe me, Miss Carlisle, so do I!" he returned smoothly. "But now lunch is ready, and afterwards I'll ask Rosa to give you some antiseptic salve to put on your arm, just in case of infection—*external* infection!"

Charlotte stiffened, and then brushing past him she walked unyieldingly back to the bungalow. She had made an absolute fool of herself again, and she wanted to cry tears of angry frustration, but instead she joined Mrs. Meredith at the table on the verandah, without even mentioning the spider bite.

In the afternoon, Mrs. Meredith and the boys rested. Charlotte wasn't sure whether Patrick Meredith rested too, so she stayed in her room, nursing her hurt pride. Even though she had closed the shutters against the glare of the sun, and a fan was working, it was incredibly hot, and she knew she would have to change her clothes again before evening.

However, as the afternoon wore on, and she went to the wardrobe to extract the apricot tunic again, she found that it had been freshly laundered, and she presumed Rosa must have done it for her. She felt very grateful, and wondered whether she might broach the subject of the dress material again with Mrs. Meredith.

She felt a sense of restlessness at her enforced confinement in the bungalow. After this morning's little escapade she didn't feel particularly enthusiastic about venturing far alone. After all, there were poisonous insects about as well as other creatures like scorpions, for example, and while she had always thought herself capable of facing any disaster, this was something outside her previous experience. She had no intention of making a fool of herself in front of Patrick Meredith again if she could help it.

Yvonne Dupré joined them for dinner that evening. When Charlotte sauntered, with assumed nonchalance, along the corridor to the verandah, she found John and Michael, Yvonne and Patrick all sitting there in the lamplight, drinking and talking together. She felt terribly *de trop*, but there was nothing she could do about it, and when Patrick rose to his feet and offered her his lounger, she accepted with as much inconsequence as she could summon. Tonight, in dark, narrow-cut trousers and a cream silk shirt, he looked tall and assured, and treated her with a kind of indifference.

She accepted a long drink of lime and lemon spliced with vodka, and then sat back in the hope that they would go on talking and ignore her. However, her wishes were doomed from the outset. Yvonne, looking rather exotic in a scarlet sari-type gown that swathed the curves of her full figure flatteringly, was obviously intensely curious about their unexpected guest, and began asking questions immediately, questions which Charlotte found it difficult not to answer.

"Tell me, Miss Carlisle," she said, "you strike me as being the kind of woman devoted to her career, would you say that was so?"

Charlotte shrugged. "Well—er—naturally I enjoy my work," she replied awkwardly.

"Yes, but is it the most important thing in your life?" Yvonne smiled charmingly. "What I am getting at is—are you not—how shall I put it?—affianced?"

Charlotte glanced uncomfortably at Patrick Meredith, leaning on the verandah rail, arms folded, watching her.

"No," she replied shortly. "I have no fiancé!"

"This is unusual, is it not?" Yvonne frowned. "Even in England women are the natural home-makers, are they not?"

Charlotte frowned, and studied her drink. "That is a fallacy, encouraged by men who treat women as —well, second-class citizens," she said quietly.

Patrick Meredith uttered an amused exclamation. "Good heavens, an emancipationist in our midst!" he exclaimed. "Are you never to stop surprising us, Miss Carlisle?"

Charlotte gave him a killing glance. "Like all men, Mr. Meredith, you ridicule anything that threatens your comfortable way of life!"

Patrick lit a cheroot. "And what particular part of my life do you threaten, Miss Carlisle?" he asked lazily.

Charlotte's cheeks burned, and Yvonne looked strangely at her. "It seems you are as feminine as all of us," she said coolly, looking up at Patrick again "Do not persist in baiting her, Patrick. She is your guest!"

Patrick sighed. "My dear Yvonne, Miss Carlisle persists in trying to prove she is something she is not. I agree she has a responsible position with this agency, though why she should have been chosen for this particular job I can't imagine, but nevertheless she is as human as the rest of us, and whether she likes it or not, she is a woman, and there's nothing she can do about it. Not if the realization drives her to distraction!" He grinned. "But I agree, I'm not acting as a good host should. Miss Carlisle, what do you think of our island, now that you've had the chance to see something of it?"

Charlotte's fingers tightened on her glass, and Michael said: "I shouldn't think she's seen much of it, Uncle Pat. She hasn't been out since—since—" he looked at his uncle, and then nodded: "—since this morning!"

Yvonne glanced at her. "Where did you go this morning, Miss Carlisle?"

Charlotte refused to look up. "I—I walked along the beach. To the headland."

"Oh, you saw the gully, then?"

"The gully? Oh, you mean that small chasm? Yes. It's very pretty." Even so, Charlotte could not suppress a shudder.

"Yes, isn't it?" Yvonne nodded. "And what did you do this afternoon?"

"Nothing." Now Charlotte looked up. "I—I assumed everyone rested."

Patrick drew on his cheroot. "We're not all lotus-eaters, you know," he remarked. "Do you play tennis? Or swim?"

Charlotte lifted her shoulders. "Both. Why?"

Yvonne patted her hand. "Tomorrow we must show you the—the rest of the island." She seemed to hesitate as she met Patrick's eyes. "We have been playing tennis this afternoon."

"In this heat?" Charlotte was horrified.

"You know what they say about mad dogs . . ." remarked Patrick, grinning. Then Mrs. Meredith appeared, and he said: "Did you go out this morning, Mother?"

Mrs. Meredith shook her head. "Why?"

"I thought you might have taken the moke along the coast, and shown Miss Carlisle Coralido."

His words were clear and concise, and at once Charlotte felt on edge.

"If Miss Carlisle wants to see Coralido, she'll have to find it for herself," retorted Mrs. Meredith coldly. "I certainly shan't encourage the development by aiding and abetting its conspirators!"

"Good lord!" Patrick raised his eyes heavenward. "Miss Carlisle isn't a conspirator! She came here on a perfectly innocent expedition to find Andrew. You can hardly blame her for that. Besides, unwittingly she has warned us what to expect, hasn't she? I mean—without her intervention we would still have been harbouring the belief that Andrew didn't intend to do anything with the place, except leave it to the jungle."

Mrs. Meredith gave an indifferent sniff. "If you ask me—" she began, only to halt uncertainly, then Yvonne changed the subject.

Charlotte was aware of a kind of reserve about all of them when the conversation reached any point of conflict, as though they knew something more than she did, and it was most annoying. Still, she consoled herself, if Andrew Meredith left Manatoa several days before her arrival, sooner or later he would be coming back, if only to find out whether she had arrived or not.

Dinner was a pleasant meal, and Charlotte managed to enjoy a little of the food tonight. Her nerves were still on edge, but the two boys, supplemented by Yvonne and Patrick, talked desultorily, and no one addressed her very often, for which she was grateful. Yvonne was pleasant enough, but she was also curious, and Charlotte had no particular desire to discuss her personal affairs amongst a crowd of veritable strangers. John and Michael were too young to care very much whether she was involved in the conversation or otherwise. They were far too interested in Patrick Meredith's description of the struggle he had once had with a shark when he was out fishing with some of the natives in a canoe.

"Actually," he went on, John and Michael completely ignoring the food on their plates as they listened with wide eyes, "some natives in the Tongan islands noose sharks, actually slot a rope about their necks and then club them to death."

Yvonne gave a shrill cry. "Really, Patrick, must you discuss such things at the table? I find it all positively nauseating!"

Patrick grinned. "You'll have to harden yourself, Yvonne. Not everything in life is as pretty as you would like it to be."

"*Chérie*, I know! I don't go around with my eyes closed. It's just that—well—" She shuddered expressively.

Patrick turned his dark eyes on Charlotte. "How about you, Miss Carlisle? Do you have a strong stomach?"

Charlotte knew he was gently amusing himself at her expense. He knew exactly how weak were her defences. But she refused to allow him to mock her again.

"I expect you mean—could I stand all the gory details," she said, putting a mouthful of fruit soufflé into her mouth deliberately. Then, swallowing the food, she continued: "When it comes to gory details I find my stomach as strong as the next person's. I've heard some men keel over at the sight of a hypodermic!"

Patrick finished his soufflé and pushed away his plate. "So they do," he nodded, leaning back in his chair, flexing his muscles. "But you wouldn't?"

"No."

"Er—you're a fearless female, then?" He bit his lip musingly.

John, who had been listening to this interchange, joined into the conversation. "Miss Carlisle suffers from—what was it you said she suffered from, Uncle Pat?"

Charlotte heaved a sigh. Of course, this was what Patrick Meredith had been angling for. And now John had given him the ideal opportunity.

But surprisingly, Patrick seemed to have changed his mind, for ignoring John's question, he said: "If we've all finished, we'll have coffee on the verandah." He looked at the two boys. "Off to bed, you two. And don't forget to wash behind your ears. You can read for half an hour and then Gran and I will come and say goodnight."

With grimaces, the boys complied, calling goodnight to Charlotte and Yvonne. The adults left the table and went out on to the verandah, and Yvonne said, puzzledly:

"What was that John meant, Patrick? About Miss Carlisle?"

Patrick glanced at Charlotte, and then shrugged. "I don't really know," he lied smoothly. "Oh, yes, I believe I said she suffered—from the heat!"

CHAPTER FOUR

THE next morning dawned bright and clear, a faint haze on the horizon indicating that it was going to be very hot. Charlotte rose early, soon after seven, and showered and dressed hastily, making her way to the verandah as quickly as she could. She had no intention of allowing Mrs. Meredith the opportunity of remarking on her late rising again.

However, when she stepped on to the verandah she found Patrick Meredith alone at the breakfast table, with evidences of vacated places all around him.

Charlotte sighed, and he looked up. "Good morning, Miss Carlisle," he said lazily, putting aside the magazine he had been reading, and indicating the place beside him. "I'll just clear these away. Rosa will be back directly with some fresh coffee, so you can share that."

Charlotte seated herself with ill grace, and he frowned as he gathered together the empty plates. "Now what's wrong," he asked impatiently. "You do want some breakfast, don't you?"

She shrugged her slim shoulders. "I wanted to be in time," she said broodingly. "I thought I would be. As it is . . ." She waved an arm towards the empty places.

He grinned and said: "John and Michael are up at six. They always go for a swim in the early morning, before breakfast."

Charlotte realized his hair was wet too. "And you?"

"Yes, me too," he agreed, and disappeared along the passage towards the back of the house. Charlotte had not seen any more of the house than the long lounge-cum-dining room and the verandah, and of course her bedroom, and she got to her feet and walked to the end of the passage, looking along it curiously. It was ridiculous really; this was the third day she had been on Manatoa, and she knew little more about the place now than she had done when she arrived with Captain Koroledo.

Patrick Meredith appeared again, and came strolling towards her. "Well," he said, "what is it?"

Charlotte scuffed her shoes moodily. "Does there have to be something?" she said ill-humouredly. "Oh—well, yes, there is something! I can't hang around the bungalow indefinitely."

"Nobody suggested that you should."

"No, but conversely, no one seems particularly keen on making any effort to get me away for a while!" She thrust her hands into the pockets of her jeans. "And I have very few clothes to wear. Your mother did say something yesterday about letting Rosa make some material up into a couple of dresses for me, but since . . ." She halted, and turned red.

"Since what? Patrick's eyes narrowed. "What's happened now? Has my mother said something to you?"

"She—well, she explained why she was so annoyed that your cousin should be endeavouring to lease Coralido," nodded Charlotte, refusing to tell him the whole of his mother's outburst. He must know already the strength of her feelings on the matter.

"I see. In no uncertain terms, no doubt," remarked Patrick, nodding to a chair. "Sit down.

Rosa is bringing you some fruit juice and some pancakes. They're delicious the way she makes them, oozing with lemon and sugar—"

"Oh, but I couldn't eat anything so fattening!" exclaimed Charlotte in alarm, and Patrick Meredith's eyes grew appraising.

"Why? You don't look particularly needful of slimming to me," he said, and she looked away from the amused look in his dark eyes.

"I know, but—well, it's causing Rosa a lot of bother!"

"Nonsense, she doesn't mind. Besides, I could eat another couple myself!" He found a clean cup and poured out the dregs of the coffee pot into it. Swallowing it, he said: "You mustn't allow my mother to intimidate you. I know perfectly well how she feels about Coralido, and I suppose I feel the same. The difference between us is that she can see no ultimate solution to the problem, and as she's much older, naturally she feels it more strongly."

Charlotte seated herself at the table and cupped her chin on her hand. "And you can see a solution to it all?" she questioned seriously.

"Let's say, while there's life there's hope," he replied evasively, and with that she had to be content.

The pancakes Rosa brought were delicious, and she couldn't resist them. The coffee, too, was aromatic and strong, and she had several cups before accepting a cigarette from her host. He seemed amused at the way she had enjoyed the meal and said:

"I suppose now all you'll want for lunch is a lettuce leaf," in a mocking tone.

"Something like that," agreed Charlotte, and relaxed.

It was very pleasant, sitting there on the verandah, a faint breeze stealing to them from the ocean that churned ceaselessly only a few hundred yards away.

"Tell me," said Patrick suddenly, "what was that about your needing some clothes? I would have thought that any of the material my mother possesses would hardly be suitable for someone of your age."

"I don't know what she has," replied Charlotte, frowning. "I was purely grateful for the chance to have anything rather than wear the same dress every evening. After all, you did say you didn't know how long I should be here, didn't you?"

Patrick lit a cheroot with his eyes on the horizon, a faraway look in their depths. Then he shrugged. "Yes, I said that," he agreed smoothly. "Now, what do you plan to do with yourself today?"

"What would your suggest?" asked Charlotte, rather sarcastically. At his words all her new-found peace of mind vanished, and she remembered with depressing clarity the boredom of yesterday. It was all right for Yvonne Dupré, she supposed, being a member of the community, and as such having access to all their activities, and obviously boredom didn't trouble her, but Charlotte thought that if she had to spend another day just sitting around the bungalow she would go mad.

She knew, too, that in the normal way the lack of activity wouldn't have troubled her. What did trouble her was her enforced sojourn on the island, and the inevitable problems that would arise if Andrew Meredith didn't return soon. It was this, combined with a sense of anxiety about Evan's reactions when he found she had disappeared, that made her feel so restless.

She looked across at Patrick, noticing inconsequently that his lashes were long and thick and successfully veiled his expression if he so desired. Just now he was studying her rather intently, and she felt the hot colour invading her cheeks again. She was not unused to the admiration of the opposite sex, but Patrick's gaze was not so much admiring as speculative, and she wondered what he was thinking. Certainly in her cotton jeans and a green T-shirt she felt anything but glamorous, her hair loose about her shoulders, and no make-up at all.

"Do I embarrass you?" he asked lazily. "Surely men have looked at you before. You're a very attractive girl."

Charlotte attempted to be as matter-of-fact as he was. "Yes," she said, "I've been looked at before. But I get the feeling that you have something different on your mind. Besides, I don't particularly like it, whatever purpose is behind it!"

Patrick drew on his cheroot. "Tell me," he said, "don't your parents object to your coming half across the world alone like this?"

Charlotte stiffened. "I'm not a child, you know."

"I know that. But conversely you're not particularly mature."

"What do you mean?"

"Simply that a more mature woman wouldn't turn a brilliant shade of tomato just because I looked at her."

Charlotte got up from the table. "You deliberately try to upset me," she exclaimed angrily.

"Why? Is there something about me that irritates you, or something?"

Patrick sighed. "All right, Miss Carlisle, cool down. By the way, what is your name? Or do you prefer formality?"

"I think in the circumstances it would be as well if we observed the formalities," she replied tautly. "After—after Mr. Meredith returns, I don't expect we shall meet again."

"Ah yes!" Patrick tipped his chair back on its hind legs. "When Andrew returns! I wonder when he will return, Miss Carlisle. Don't you find yourself wondering that?"

Charlotte felt incensed. Constantly she had this feeling with Patrick Meredith that he was simply playing with her, teasing her and tormenting her, and she was helpless to defy him. She wasn't even sure whether there was anything to defy, but he must know how he disturbed her, and it amused him to tantalize her with statements that aroused both awareness and curiosity inside her.

"You must know I wonder that all the time!" she snapped.

Patrick got to his feet. "All right, all right. I know—I'm annoying you again. Well, let me see, how can we entertain you today?"

"You don't have to entertain me, Mr. Meredith!" she replied angrily, uncaring for the moment of the fate she was securing for herself.

Patrick shrugged. "You don't want to come with me this morning? To the plantation? I thought you might be interested to meet Yvonne's father, and several of the other wives here."

Charlotte chewed her lips indecisively. "I don't know," she said churlishly.

71

"Please yourself. I thought you told me earlier you would like to see the island!"

"So I did. But . . . well. . . ." Charlotte lifted her shoulders. "Please, Mr. Meredith, be honest with me! Is there a way I could reach Suva?"

"Sure!" Patrick stubbed out his cheroot.

"What?" Charlotte's eyes were wide. "How?"

"You could swim," he replied laconically. And then as Charlotte gasped with indignation, he said: "Ah, here come John and Mike. Want to come down to the plantation, boys?"

The boys were eager, prancing about excitedly, and Mrs. Meredith appeared, ostensibly to see what all the noise was about. When she saw Charlotte she frowned.

"Oh, you're up, Miss Carlisle!"

"Yes, and she's had breakfast," said Patrick smoothly. "And now she's coming with me, down to the plantation."

"But ought you—I mean—Patrick, you know what I mean!"

Patrick gave his mother a wry smile. "Yes, I ought. Now, be good! Come on—er—Miss Carlisle. You didn't tell me what your Christian name was, did you?"

Seething, but unwilling to remain with Mrs. Meredith, Charlotte followed Patrick and the two boys round to the rear of the long building where, in a belt of trees, there was the double garage which served as a playroom for the boys in wet weather. This information Patrick imparted casually, as they walked towards a dust-covered LandRover.

"The boys," said Charlotte tentatively. "If they're not yours, then . . ."

"They're my sister's—Andrea. She and her husband are in the process of divorcing one another."

"I see." Charlotte nodded, glancing sympathetically towards the children who had jumped into the vehicle, and were blowing the horn loudly.

"Don't sound so cut up about it," remarked Patrick dryly. "It's probably the best thing that could happen to them!"

"Whatever do you mean?" Charlotte was horrified.

"Andrea and Simon never got on. They were always fighting. No one ever won, of course. It was just a bloody mess! John and Mike are better out of it!" He glanced her way. "Do you disapprove? Are you one of those people who believe that a bad marriage is better for the children than no marriage at all?"

"I haven't really thought about it," she replied, shrugging.

Patrick swung himself into the Land-Rover. "Haven't you? Then perhaps you should. It's something a person like you might have to face!"

"What do you mean?"

"I mean that Andrea is like you. She's an emancipationist, too. She wants her career, and she means to have it, even if it means sacrificing the marriage which eleven years ago meant everything to her!"

Charlotte climbed in beside him, as the boys scrambled into the back. "Well, I have no plans for getting married!" she said shortly.

"No? Of course, you're the ultimate product of your kind, aren't you? You'll avoid the mistakes Andrea made, and then you'll have none of the problems to face later. No helpless children to fight over!"

"I don't think you can make any judgments on me, Mr. Meredith!" Charlotte exclaimed angrily. "And it may surprise you to know that despite my desire for equal rights, I want to get married one day, and have children of my own. I merely meant I had no immediate plans for getting married!"

Patrick did not reply. He merely gave her a mocking glance before turning on the engine of the Land Rover. They drove away down the small drive that led on to the track which in one direction led to the sea, the way Charlotte was already familiar with, and in the other into the jungle. It was this direction they took, travelling under a green cavern of foliage, that shut out most of the sun. There was a damp musty smell of earth and rotting vegetation, and the sometimes heady perfume of the flamboyant flowers they passed made Charlotte feel rather sick. Even so, she was amazed that such exotic blossoms should flower, out of sight of the sun.

Sometimes the thick interweaving of parasitic plants spread across the road to be crushed by the wheels of the vehicle, and Charlotte forgot her indignation for a moment and said: "I should imagine it's difficult to keep this road clear of vegetation, isn't it?"

Patrick nodded. "It's the same all over the island. It's an almost daily chore to chop back the jungle and keep some semblance of order. Everything grows with such abundance that it's practically impossible to win. In the plantation we employ men to keep the undergrowth clear so that when the nuts fall they are easily gathered. One of the most tenacious plants is the lantana. Have you heard of it?"

"Lantana? Oh, yes. It's quite pretty, isn't it? I believe I've heard of people cultivating it."

"Yes. They do in New Zealand. But it's a pest here."

"How long does it take to grow coconuts? I mean, do the palms produce fruit more or less straight away?"

"No, nothing so simple. Palms take about six years to grow to maturity, that is to say when they start bearing the nuts. Then a nut takes several more years to grow and ripen. Fortunately, we have palms at different stages of development and as nuts can fall all the year round we're usually well employed. The full season is usually June to September, and then we're really kept going."

"I see. It's interesting, isn't it?" Charlotte sighed.

Patrick looked at her a trifle dryly. "Do you really find it so? Or can you see this development company going in for conducted tours of the island plantation, with a guide droning out the patter?"

Charlotte compressed her lips. "Please, don't you start!" she exclaimed. "And no matter what you think, I am interested." She bit her lip. "Tell me about the people who live here. How many white people are there?"

"Well, there are the Duprés, of course. Yvonne will have told you her father is a doctor?" And at Charlotte's nod, he went on: "Then there's Sam Morris and his wife. Sam was once my father's partner. In the days when Gordon was selling his land, my father didn't have the ready cash to pay him. Sam came in on the deal on the understanding that when my father could afford to buy back the land, he would let him do so. My father repaid the loan years ago, but Sam stays on. He likes it here. His family are all grown up and married and live in various parts of the world, but he stays here. He likes to help about the office and he's pretty good with engines. And we like him."

Charlotte smiled. "He sounds nice."

"Oh, he is. Now who else is there? There's the padre, Mr. Duncan, and his wife. He's not the island padre, or anything like that. We couldn't afford a full-time clergyman here, but when he retired, he was a friend of my grandfather's, he came here and decided to stay. Actually, he performed the ceremony when my sister and her husband got married, in the lounge of the bungalow that my father owned then. It was quite an exciting affair. Of course, since then we've constructed a new bungalow."

"Aren't there any young people?" she queried, frowning.

"Oh, yes. There's Don Perdom, and Jim Ferris. Don is my second-in-command. He answered an advertisement we put in an Australian paper several years ago. He wasn't married then, just engaged, but he came for a few months, and then went back and brought over his new wife. Jim is in charge of all the paper work. He's not married, although he's been engaged a few times. Finally, there's Grant Summers. He and his wife run the school for the children here on the island. There are quite a few of them, including the Summers' own children, Linda and Steven. They're twins of—I think they're four. At any rate they don't attend school yet. The Perdoms have a baby, too."

"Quite a community!" said Charlotte, in surprise. "Somehow I never expected it."

"What did you expect?"

Charlotte shrugged. "To be quite honest I imagined that this Andrew Meredith was the only white man on an island completely uncultivated apart from his section. Then of course Captain Koroledo of the *Fijian Star* told me that there was a plantation here, imagining of course that it was you I wanted to see."

"I see. Tell me, how did Andrew come to offer Coralido to you?"

Charlotte bent her head, and did not reply.

"Oh, I'm sorry," said Patrick, rather sardonically. "Does that come under the heading of classified information?"

"No, not really. But—well, I don't think I should discuss his affairs with you."

"Perhaps you're right. After all, I warn you I'm like my mother in one respect, and that is I'll do everything in my power to prevent this development."

They had left the jungle behind them now and were travelling along a road between tall hedges of tauhunu, an impenetrable shrub standing some twenty feet in height. Charlotte was still amazed at the wild untrammelled abundance of the shrubs, and the heavy bulk of the trees that struggled to raise their branches above them. Pointing to the broad trunk of one of the trees, she said: "What is that, and why does it look so twisted?"

"That's a tamanu," replied John, bouncing up and down in his seat. "Isn't it, Uncle Pat?"

His uncle nodded, and John went on: "The trunk is twisted because years ago, in a violent hurricane, it was almost wrenched out by its roots. Some trees were torn out, weren't they, Uncle Pat?"

Charlotte shivered. Until now the beauty of the island had successfully concealed the fact that where there was violent heat there were also violent storms, and she glanced at Patrick as she said: "Do you have many hurricanes?"

"Some," he replied. "Not all the savage kind that John is talking about. That particular hurricane caused a tidal wave that destroyed homes and crops and livestock. Fortunately they occur very infrequently."

"Oh!" Charlotte swallowed hard.

"Don't worry," remarked Patrick dryly. "We're only on the fringe of the hurricane season at the moment, and it's hardly likely you'll be here long enough to be involved in one. Besides, we usually have plenty of warning. There are those among the islanders who believe they can foretell the coming of a storm weeks in advance."

"And can they?"

"Who can tell? I'm an islander myself and I'm prepared to take their word for it."

"Old Mayangi says the sea boils!" exclaimed Michael dramatically, but Patrick gave him a quelling look.

"That's enough, Mike," he said firmly. "You've never witnessed a hurricane, so you're merely quoting gossip in an attempt to frighten Miss Carlisle." He glanced at Charlotte with a wry smile. "I rather think our guest has a vivid enough imagination as it is!"

Charlotte refused to meet his mocking eyes, and instead gave her attention to her surroundings again.

They were approaching a collection of small dwellings, little bigger than huts, with palm-thatched roofs and gaps in the sides in place of windows. The village, which was what Charlotte realized it was, was quite extensive, standing in a small valley where a stream widened into a shallow river. The stream seemed to come tumbling down the hillside from nowhere and then disappeared through a cleft of rock.

"That's the waterfall you saw at the gully," explained Patrick, smiling at some women who stopped their task of washing clothes in the stream to wave at them. Dozens of children swarmed around, mostly naked, and staring curiously at Charlotte.

Charlotte turned in her seat as they splashed through the stream and came out at the other side before a stretch of open land, cultivated and planted with rows of coconut palms. There was an unnatural regimented quality about the trees, much different from the riotous abandon to be found elsewhere.

"This is the start of the plantation," said Michael, speaking for the first time. "There's a lot of it. It stretches right to the other side of the island, doesn't it, Uncle Patrick?"

"Is that where we're going?" asked Charlotte, noticing that now the village was disappearing behind them, and they were engulfed in trees. The track was rough and mud-packed, but because there had been rain recently it was firm and not dusty, for which she was grateful.

"No," replied Patrick, changing gear to negotiate a steep rise in the gradient. "We're going to the south side of the island. The plantation buildings are there, and so is the school. The Summers' house is near the school, and Jim Ferris has a bungalow nearby. Sometimes Jean Summers gives him his meals. He has an Indian servant, like Rosa, but not so efficient, and certainly not such a good cook."

Charlotte nodded, glad she had been prevailed upon to accompany him. There was so much to see, and so much beauty in the landscape. She could recall the stream in detail, still seeing the wide stepping stones used by the women to negotiate its width, while small blue flowers, like those she had seen in the gully, grew in its dry crevices.

"Just out of curiosity," she said, speaking quietly, "where is Coralido?"

Patrick put the Land Rover back into top gear, and they crested the rise and began to travel down a twisting slope towards the coast again. Ahead of them was a mass of greenery, interspersed here and there with patches of colour from the hibiscus trees, and Charlotte caught her breath at its beauty, the cobalt blue of the sky melting into a sea like velvet. Palms formed a frame for the picture, and she wished she had the talent to capture such an exotic landscape on canvas, as so many artists had tried to do. And yet she had the feeling that it would be impossible to convey such brilliance of colour, such clarity of detail, to any artificial facsimile, and only the real thing could excite and enthrall and enchant.

So enthralled was she that when Patrick said: "On the north side of the island," she found it difficult to assimilate what he meant. Frowning at her expression, he said: "Coralido! You asked me where it was."

"Oh—oh, yes!" Charlotte felt embarrassed. "It's all so beautiful! Quite unbelievably so. I can understand why—what was the man's name?— Sam, something or other, why he wanted to stay! I should imagine it could be like a fever in the blood!"

Patrick seemed surprised at her perspicacity. "It is," he agreed, looking at her for a moment. "You describe it perfectly. A fever in the blood! I must remember that."

Charlotte felt her colour deepening, and she quickly changed the subject and began asking about the kilns for drying the copra, but she was conscious of his speculative gaze on her more than once.

Suddenly they came upon the plantation buildings, mostly single-storied dwellings, obviating the dangers of high winds, Charlotte assumed. The kilns were tall and dark, and unattractive, but the rambling shrubs successfully concealed them from sight of the houses that mostly overlooked a small bay, edged by the pink-hued coral of the reef.

Patrick parked the Land Rover near the kilns, and the boys scrambled out. Some men were working nearby, and stopped to view their visitors, but when they saw Patrick they merely nodded a greeting and continued working.

"Come on," said Patrick. "The schoolhouse is this way. It should be time for morning break. We'll see if Grant and Jean can offer us coffee before we go looking for Don and Jim."

The schoolhouse was a long low hut, full of chattering schoolchildren, all black and round-faced, and excited that their lessons should have had such a welcome interruption. Some of them launched themselves at Patrick, shouting hello and asking him questions at the tops of their voices. A young woman pushed her way through the crowd, called for order, clapped her hands and said that the children could have a ten-minute break. Then she smiled at Patrick and said:

"What's the meaning of this? Coming interrupting my work?" in a bantering tone.

81

"I've brought—Miss Carlisle to meet you, Jean," said Patrick easily. "Er—Miss Carlisle, this is Mrs. Summers."

"Oh, please call me Jean, everyone does," exclaimed the young woman laughingly. She was small and rather plump in appearance with dark wavy hair, cut short for coolness. In a cotton dress and sandals, she looked young to be the mother of four-year-old twins. Charlotte wondered where they were.

"How do you do?" she said, in answer to Jean Summers' greeting, and then, because it was obviously expected of her, she went on: "My name is Charlotte."

Patrick grinned rather mockingly, and Charlotte gave him an impatient glance, but Jean Summers noticed nothing amiss.

"Charlotte," she said. "It's a nice name. We're all very informal here. It would be ridiculous in a small community like ours to stand on ceremony, wouldn't it?"

"I suppose so," agreed Charlotte shortly.

The boys were amongst the schoolchildren, apparently well pleased with their companions, and Jean said: "Come on, we'll have some coffee. That is what you came for, isn't it, Patrick?"

Patrick nodded. "Of course. I'm in the process of showing—er—Miss Carlisle the island. We thought we would look you up first."

Jean Summers frowned at his use of Charlotte's surname, but said nothing. Instead, she gave the children orders to be back at their desks in a quarter of an hour, and led the way through the belt of trees that flanked the schoolhouse to where another low bungalow was built, on a rise overlooking the cove below, where several dinghies rocked on their moorings.

"What a lovely view!" exclaimed Charlotte, as they mounted the steps of the verandah, and Jean Summers indicated that they should sit while she went to see about the coffee.

"Yes, isn't it?" she smiled. "By the way, Pat, Grant has taken the children over to Taiwanu to—" But Patrick interrupted her.

"Let me help you with that coffee," he said, and leaving Charlotte alone, he accompanied the other woman into the house. Charlotte felt a ridiculous sense of pique. It was all very well knowing she was an unwanted intruder on the island, but she didn't much like being made to feel that there were things too private for her to unwittingly overhear and register. And yet in the Land Rover coming here hadn't she herself refused to discuss Andrew Meresith's side of this with Patrick? And hadn't Patrick every right therefore to protect his own interests, in much the same way as she was trying to protect hers?

She sighed, watching the antics of a brightly coloured bird in the leaves of a nearby pandanus tree, and wished she had a cigarette. She wondered what Jean Summers and Patrick were discussing in the intimacy of the kitchen. Was it anything to do with herself, or Andrew Meredith? Or was it a more personal problem? She sighed again. She was beginning to get far too interested in the community's affairs. If she wasn't careful she would find herself seeing Patrick Meredith's side of the affair, and that would be disastrous. It would prove once and for all that she was allowing her emotions to rule her common sense. All right, it was a beautiful island, and obviously the people who lived here were happy and contented, but everyone, sooner or later, had to face the complications that civilization brought. Why, in England people were continually being up-rooted from their homes, removed from the surroundings they had always known and loved and placed instead in monolithic structures called flats, far away from the street, and from the easy intimacy of community life. At least these people here were not threatened with mass evacuation. All that would happen would be that a small holiday village would be built on this patch of land called Coralido, and its occupants would be as remote from the rest of the island as this community was remote from the bright lights and noisy bustle of Suva.

But would they? argued a small voice inside her. Wouldn't it only be a matter of time before the villagers in that native village they had passed became curious about the new settlement and went to investigate. Would the super-luxury of the Belmain Estates development arouse interest or dissatisfaction inside them? Might they gravitate away from the comfortable life of the plantation, in search of something that hitherto had been alien to them? Was this what Patrick Meredith was afraid of? This and the possible invasion of his privacy, albeit unwittingly?

Charlotte's thoughts were chaotic. It was impossible to be here, to see the plantation as it was run, and not be aware of its limitations and its advantages.

The mesh door behind her opened, and Patrick emerged carrying a tray, followed by Jean Summers, who was looking rather pleased with herself. Charlotte was aware of a stirring of emotion at that look on Jean's face. As yet she was unaware of what the

feeling portended, and she was furious with hersel
for feeling a kind of possessiveness towards Patrick
Meredith. Until now, even with Yvonne Dupré, she
had not sensed that kind of sensation, and it was not
pleasant to know that she was beginning to identify
herself here.

Shrugging these thoughts away, she refused the
small cakes Jean proffered her, and instead said,
rather jerkily: "Have you a cigarette?" to Patrick.

Looking slightly amused, Patrick offered her his
case, then said: "You're looking rather hot and
bothered. What's happened now?"

Charlotte stiffened her shoulders. "Nothing's
happened," she denied swiftly. Then to Jean Summers: "You have twins?"

Jean glanced at Patrick, then nodded. "A boy
and a girl. Linda and Steven, they're four. Unfortunately they're not here at the moment. They
would have liked to have met you. Perhaps you
could come another day . . ."

"Thank you, that would be nice." Charlotte drew
on her cigarette rather frustratedly.

"Of course, if Andrew returns you may not have
time." Jean glanced surreptitiously at Patrick.
"You're from England, Pat says."

"I live in London," replied Charlotte shortly,
wondering what else Patrick Meredith had said.

"With your parents?" questioned Jean.

"No. My parents were killed in the earthquakes
in Yugoslavia. They were on holiday at the time."

Jean gave a sympathetic sigh. "How dreadful for
you! And have you no brothers or sisters?"

"One brother," said Charlotte.

"Is he married?"

"Yes," returned Charlotte, beginning to resent this persistent questioning. Really, it was like the third degree! Had Patrick Meredith asked Jean to ask all these questions knowing how reluctant she was to talk to him about personal matters?

"And haven't you any inclinations towards the married state?" asked Jean, apparently unaware of her guest's abbreviated replies.

Charlotte sighed. "I have my work!" she said bleakly.

"Miss Carlisle takes her work very seriously," remarked Patrick, entering the conversation.

Charlotte looked his way. "My work is serious!" she said coldly.

"Of course!" Patrick gave a mocking gesture. "Believe me, I don't doubt that!"

Charlotte compressed her lips. It was infuriating to feel so helpless.

Later Patrick rose, stretching. "We must go, Jean." He smiled. "Send the boys to Jim's place. They'll find us there or in the office."

"All right," Jean nodded, and when she got up, Charlotte got up too. She was still feeling rather like a child who has accompanied an adult on an outing, and she felt the sense of outrage that she should experience such feelings. After all, there was nothing intimidating about Jean Summers, and Patrick Meredith simply enjoyed amusing himself at her expense. Even so, the feeling persisted that they were concealing something from her, and she wondered desperately what Evan would have done if confronted by the same situation.

Jean said: "Do come and see us again, Charlotte, if you have the time. When the children are here, of course."

"I will, if I can," replied Charlotte, taking the woman's outstretched hand politely. "Mr. Meredith doesn't think there'll be a ship for quite some time, so I expect I shall be able to."

Jean looked at Patrick. "Yes, well, we'll look forward to that," she said, smiling benevolently.

As Charlotte and Patrick crossed the stretch of turf between the Summers' bungalow and that belonging to Jim Ferris, she halted and said: "When we meet Mr. Ferris I should be obliged if you would refrain from acting as though I were half-witted or something!" Her tone was hot and angry.

"Half-witted?" echoed Patrick, in surprise. "What in heaven's name are you talking about now?" He leaned his back against the trunk of a huge palm. "You're extremely touchy! When have I acted as though you were half-witted?"

Charlotte shook her head. "You must have realized by now that I know you're deliberately keeping something from me!" she stormed. "Tell me truthfully, is Andrew Meredith on the island?"

"Andrew? Here?" Patrick took out a cheroot and lit it carefully. "Whatever gave you that idea?"

"You did! Oh, stop playing for time, is it true?"

"No, it is not true. Andrew Meredith is, as far as I know, either in Suva or on his way there. Maybe even on his way back."

Charlotte gritted her teeth. "Then why do you all act as though there's something I ought to know but don't?"

"Do we act like that?"

"You know you do!" stormed Charlotte, allowing some of her frustration free vent at last. "Your mother starts sentences and then doesn't finish them. Rosa isn't allowed to start talking to me, and now Mrs. Summers behaves as though intrigue was part of her ordinary daily life!"

Patrick grinned, undisturbed by her anger. "You're imagining things," he remarked lazily. "Now come on! I imagine Jim can hear voices and he'll be wondering what in hell I'm doing to you."

Charlotte compressed her lips, and thrusting her hands into the pockets of her jeans she trudged her feet towards the verandah. She was upset and somehow unhappy, and the knowledge that Patrick found it all a huge joke had everything to do with it. Why couldn't he act like his mother? she asked herself impatiently. At least her antagonism was a normal reaction. His was not. And she was completely impotent to do anything about it. Oh, hurry up, Evan, she thought inwardly; Come soon, or I shall become so involved I shan't be able to do anything objectively.

Jim Ferris was working in his living room, a long room that stretched from front to back of the bungalow, with a dining area at the far end. He was using a portable typewriter, but looked up welcomingly as Patrick pushed open the mesh door. His eyes went past Patrick to Charlotte, and he smiled admiringly.

"Well, hello," he said, getting to his feet. "Do you want something, or is this a social call?"

Patrick introduced Charlotte, calling her Miss Carlisle, and then he said: "It's social really. I've been showing Miss Carlisle a little of the island."

Jim nodded. He was a tall broad young man, with thick red hair and a bushy beard and moustache. Beside him Patrick looked very lean and very dark.

"And what do you think of the place?" Jim Ferris asked, stroking his beard. "Could you fancy this kind of life?"

Charlotte ran her tongue over her lips. "Well, I should imagine it would depend on the circumstances," she replied evasively. "But I do think it's very beautiful, and I should imagine it would be easy to fall in love with the place."

"A tactful answer!" remarked Jim, grinning. "Will you have some coffee, Patrick?"

"Not now, thanks. I have to go and find Don, and I want to see Raratonga."

"You're not going straight away, surely?"

"Why not?"

"Because I haven't had a chance to get to know our charming visitor," protested Jim, shaking his head. "You go and do what you have to do, and—er—Miss Carlisle can stay here for half an hour. I'll entertain her gladly."

Charlotte smiled. It was good to feel back in recognizable situations again. Jim Ferris she could understand and like.

Patrick hesitated, a scowl marring his usually attractive features, and Charlotte wondered again why he hesitated to leave her alone with anyone, if that was what it was.

"Do you want to stay, Miss Carlisle?" he asked, looking at her.

Charlotte shrugged. "If you like. After all, if you have some work to do, it might be as well if I were out of the way. I wouldn't want to—well, overhear anything I shouldn't!"

Patrick chewed his lip for a moment, then strode to the door. "Very well, I'll be back in a short while. If the boys come, keep them here, will you?" This to Jim Ferris.

Jim grinned. "As chaperons?" he asked jokingly, but Patrick did not laugh.

After he had gone, Jim suggested they might have some coffee after all, and he summoned his housekeeper, whom he addressed as Josepha, and asked her to bring some in.

Charlotte found him easy to talk to, and sitting at the rear of the house, where the back stretch of garden led towards the flattened area beside the kilns, they could see the men working nearby, and watch their labours. They saw Patrick, too, going into one of the kilns with another man, a dark-skinned islander who Jim told her was Raratonga, the chief of the workmen.

"Tell me," said Jim suddenly, "why is Andrew doing this to Pat?"

Charlotte shrugged her shoulders. "As I don't know Andrew Meredith I really couldn't say," she replied honestly.

"They were at school together," said Jim, pouring himself more coffee. "Pat's father paid for Andrew's education, did you know that? And this is how he repays their kindness!" There was anger in his voice.

Charlotte sighed. "Mrs. Meredith told me the story. She's very bitter."

"With every reason," said Jim, offering her a cigarette. "It was hardly their fault that Gordon Meredith squandered his inheritance. After all, he was never interested in the island, and he wanted the money more. John would have loaned him money, but Gordon insisted that he wanted no loans. Eventually he would have disposed of all the land, but unfortunately he died and young Andrew decided to make trouble."

Charlotte shook her head. "It's difficult for me to live here with Patrick Meredith and his mother knowing I'm virtually on the opposite side of the fence."

"I imagine it would be. However, if Pat wants to keep you here, that's his affair!"

Charlotte frowned. "That's a strange thing to say, Mr. Ferris."

"What?"

"That—that—" Charlotte's voice quivered a little—"that Patrick Meredith should want to keep me here; he—he has no choice!" She swallowed nervously. "Has he?"

Jim Ferris moved restlessly. "It was just an expression," he muttered gruffly, shuffling his papers. "I mean—obviously, you weren't to blame, and he could hardly throw you out with no place to go!"

Charlotte clenched her hands into fists. "Oh, honestly," she cried, "I feel as though I'm knocking my head against a brick wall!"

Jim Ferris looked troubled. "Now why?"

"Well!" Charlotte turned away sighing. "Just as I think I'm getting somewhere—I reach a dead end!"

Jim Ferris looked uncomfortable. "Look, Miss Carlisle, please don't read anything into my stupid meanderings."

"Why?" Charlotte swung round. "Are you afraid your boss will find out you've said too much and you'll get fired!"

Jim Ferris pushed back his chair. "Honestly, Miss Carlisle, this is ridiculous! I didn't say anything!"

"You did, you know," said Charlotte, chewing her lip. "In fact I'm pretty certain now that there is a way off this island, and what's more it has something to do with somewhere called Taiwanu!"

"You're crazy!" exclaimed Jim, shaking his head. "Look, let me get you some more coffee. I think the heat—"

"No, thank you," Charlotte interrupted him, and getting up from her seat she walked to the other end of the room, looking down at the bay with its small boats rocking in the faint breeze. "Tell me," she said, "do you own a dinghy?"

Apparently relieved that she had changed the subject, Jim Ferris joined her, pointing out his boat with some pride. They discussed the craft, and the possible accomplishments of the outrigger canoes that the natives used, and after a while Jim relaxed completely, obviously thinking Charlotte had abandoned her ideas of finding a way to leave Manatoa.

But inside Charlotte seethed with emotions, an overwhelming sense of anger against Patrick Meredith dominating all other feelings. If she was right, if there was some other way to leave Manatoa, then she would go into this development scheme with all the will in the world. Any sympathy she might have felt for him was banished by the indignation that swamped her. If it were true and she had been wasting these days then he would pay dearly for his insolence. She must never allow herself to forget the way he had deliberately led her into betraying confidences to him at the start of their association, and if he thought that by introducing her to the community in general he could allay the urgency of her mission, he was mistaken. He would find that he was not dealing with one of the placid island women, who seemed perfectly content to sit around making no effort to control their own destinies. She was here as the representative of the Evan Hunter Agency, and somehow she must get to the other side of Manatoa and discover for herself just what he was hiding.

CHAPTER FIVE

PATRICK drove Charlotte and the two boys back to the Merediths' bungalow for lunch, declining Jim Ferris's invitation to eat there. Charlotte was not dismayed. She was looking forward to the afternoon when she might have an opportunity to explore alone. If only she could get control of the Land Rover, she might stand a chance. But if Patrick Meredith had something to hide he would hardly be likely to hand over to her the chance to find out what that something was.

Nevertheless, as they ate lunch on the verandah in company with Mrs. Meredith, she said:

"Would it be possible for me to borrow the Land Rover this afternoon? I mean—I realize you have work to do, and I could easily explore alone." She glanced at John and Michael's expectant faces. "Maybe the boys could come with me."

Patrick pared an orange, and then smiled, rather regretfully. "I'm sorry, Miss Carlisle, but it would be out of the question to allow you to explore Manatoa unaccompanied—even with John and Michael," he amended when he saw their mouths open ready to protest. "You don't know Manatoa at all, and naturally there are things you might encounter which might frighten—or upset you!"

"I'm sure John and Michael are quite capable of advising me," said Charlotte, rather impatiently. "After all, I have been here some time now, and I haven't yet had the opportunity to see Coralido for myself."

Mrs. Meredith sniffed. "You can hardly expect us to put ourselves out to help you, Miss Carlisle," she said shortly.

"That's my point, I don't," replied Charlotte charmingly. "I thought this way I could see the land for myself, without troubling anyone."

"No," said Patrick Meredith quite clearly, smiling at her infuriatingly. "I'm sorry. However, I'll endeavour to take you there myself perhaps tomorrow."

"Thank you!" Charlotte's tone was sarcastic, and she compressed her lips angrily, sighing.

"Besides," went on Patrick disarmingly, "Yvonne has invited you to visit her this afternoon. You did say you liked tennis, didn't you?"

Charlotte wrinkled her nose. "Oh, very well," she said, with ill-grace.

Leaving the table, she walked to the verandah rail and viewed the shimmering heat with some misgivings. She contemplated declining the visit to the Duprés' and endeavouring to make her own way around the island, but such thoughts melted in the heat of the sun. However could she attempt to walk far in this? She would be exhausted in no time. Even the thought of a game of tennis was a daunting one. No, for today at least she must abandon her ideas, and appear to accept the situation. There was no point in arousing Patrick Meredith's suspicions unnecessarily. She would only be allowed one attempt to make any kind of expedition, so that attempt must prove successful or she would have merely wasted her time.

Even so, despite her misgivings, she enjoyed the afternoon at the Duprés'. She met Don Perdom and his young wife, and their adorable baby, Samantha,

95

and as the Duprés had a swimming pool, it was possible to enjoy the tennis with the prospect of a cooling dip afterwards. Simon Dupré, Yvonne's father, was a man in his early forties, with greying dark hair, and grey eyes, and looked considerably younger than Charlotte had expected.

Charlotte had had perforce to wear her trousers again, but Yvonne lent her a bathing suit, and also revealed that Patrick had mentioned her shortage of dresses. She offered two lengths of material for Charlotte to take back for Rosa to run up for her. One was a deep blue poplin, and the other a kind of embroidered lace over green satin, rather elaborate for Charlotte's taste, but pretty all the same. Charlotte thanked Yvonne enthusiastically, embarrassed when the French girl refused payment.

"Don't be silly," exclaimed Yvonne, shaking her head. They were in Yvonne's bedroom, a pretty room in pink and white, that suited her personality. "That has all been taken care of."

Charlotte wondered how, and said: "If Mr. Meredith has paid for the material, then I would rather you accepted the money from me, and returned it to him," rather awkwardly.

Yvonne viewed her strangely, and Charlotte saw the glimmer of something like annoyance in the other girl's eyes. "Please, Miss Carlisle, Patrick would hardly consider providing your wardrobe as any part of his responibilities towards you, would he?"

Charlotte felt uncomfortable now. "I know, but —well, I don't understand what you mean—about the money!"

Yvonne's eyes were coldly distant now. "We do not buy things here for cash, Miss Carlisle, over the counter as you do in England. Here we are a community, and a community shares its expenses accordingly. The cost of the dress material will be engulfed in other accounts." Then she studied Charlotte carefully. "Miss Carlisle, I hope you won't take this amiss, but it may be that your enforced stay here, on Manatoa, living in Patrick's house as his guest, has—well, afforded you an intimacy with him, which to an obviously inexperienced girl like yourself might conceivably be construed as something more than mere courtesy—"

"Oh, please!" exclaimed Charlotte hotly. "You—you—well, you couldn't be more wrong—"

"Oh, I know," said Yvonne, rather haughtily. "Do not imagine, Miss Carlisle, that I do not trust my—well, Patrick. On the contrary, your presence here alarms me not one iota. No—it is you, and only you, who I am concerned about."

Charlotte felt slightly aghast at the heartless way Yvonne had dismissed her, and naturally even slightly hurt. Until now her relationship with Yvonne had seemed normal and friendly, and now suddenly Yvonne was endeavouring to make known to her something which had been apparent from that first morning after her arrival.

"I'm sorry if you felt I was in some way abusing my position here," Charlotte said, rather stiffly.

Yvonne assumed her usual friendly expression. "And I am sorry, too," she said, linking her arm with Charlotte's. "But your assumption that Patrick should even suggest paying for your clothes caught me on the raw—is that what you say? Yes, I suppose where he is concerned I have become a little possessive."

Charlotte managed to assume a casual expression, too, but she could not help the slight feeling of pique that Yvonne's words had aroused in her. It was one thing to be accused of attempting to assume on a relationship, but quite another to be dismissed as so uninteresting as to be absolutely harmless. Charlotte, was only human, and despite her independence, she still hoped she was attractive, purely as a woman. However, this was no time or place to put that particular theory into operation, and instead she joined Yvonne's father, allowing him to hold her in conversation to the exclusion of everyone else. He was a very pleasant man, and she found it easy to talk to him. He was not young and slightly immature like Jim Ferris, and his age seemed of less importance than his personality. He told Charlotte about the work he was doing and the common ailments among the Fijians and the Indians, and offered to show her the complex layout of his laboratory if she cared to come again.

A shadow fell across them as they sat by the swimming pool in comfortable beach chairs, and looking up, Charlotte saw Patrick.

"Time to go," he said, his eyes veiled by his thick lashes. "I have to call on Jim as we go back."

Charlotte gave a regretful smile to Yvonne's father, thanked Yvonne again for the dress material, waved to the others, and then accompanied Patrick to the Land Rover. All of a sudden she was intensely conscious of him as a man, of the width of his shoulders and the tanned muscularity of his legs, and she felt annoyed that Yvonne should have promoted that awareness by her ridiculous possessiveness.

In the vehicle she kept as far away from him as she could, deliberately giving her attention to the scenery, and Patrick said at last:

"Something troubling you. What is it?"

Charlotte shook her head. "Nothing," she said shortly.

"Oh, come on, I may not have known you long, but I can tell when something has upset you. Was it Simon? Did he tell you what he thought about Belmain Estates?"

"Simon? Oh, you mean Mr. Dupré. No. I like him. I enjoyed talking to him."

Patrick looked slightly impatient. "Then it must have been Yvonne. Did she make some comment about the material she has given you? I can assure you she's not short of clothes!"

"Oh, I'm sure she's not!" exclaimed Charlotte hotly.

"Then what is it? Surely whatever she said can't have caused this absolute withdrawal from association!"

Charlotte lifted her shoulders, and Patrick wrenched the wheel of the Land Rover round savagely, swinging off the path they had been travelling, and instead penetrating a thick cavern of jungle that seemed dark and endless, so that for a heart-shaking moment Charlotte wondered where he intended taking her.

However, after a few minutes they emerged into the sunlight again, and found themselves on a narrow track beside a tumbling stream, that curved down towards the coastline to a part of the island Charlotte had never seen before. Between them and the sea was a valley, and they plunged down its slope, through the undergrowth that covered the road in places, through groves of bananas and oranges, growing in wild profusion, untended and unpicked, or so it seemed to Charlotte from the fruit that lay wasting beneath the trees.

They climbed out of the valley, close to where the hinterland rose to an impressive peak, whose name Charlotte would have liked to ask, but didn't, and then drove down through another belt of jungle to where a high, interlaced wooden fence blocked their passage.

"There it is!" he muttered, sliding out of the Land Rover and throwing out his hand in a dramatic gesture, "the place you most wanted to visit: Coralido, in all its wilderness!"

Charlotte stared at Patrick for a moment, then stared ahead at the overgrown waste before her. This was Coralido; this was the place that Andrew Meredith hoped to lease to the Belmain Estates company. It was fantastic! Obviously no one, not even Evan, could have imagined anything as coarse and uncultivated as this.

She climbed out of the vehicle and walked to the fence.

"Can we—can we go inside?" She looked back at Patrick. "Is it possible?"

"If we climb the fence and penetrate the jungle we might reach the house by nightfall," remarked Patrick sarcastically, and then repenting: "Oh, I suppose we can push our way through. But we mustn't take long. It will be dark soon, and I'm sure even you are not brave enough to face the night insects without being able to see them!"

Charlotte made a face at his mockery, but a sense of excitement was rising in her. This was adventure, this was what life was all about, and just now she wouldn't have exchanged places with anybody.

With agile movements, Patrick vaulted the fence, swinging himself over with one hand, leaving her gasping on the other side.

"But how am I . . . I mean . . ." She sighed, and he grinned.

"Oh, come on, Miss Carlisle," he mocked her. "What would any hot-blooded male do in the same circumstances?"

Charlotte ignored his amusement, and struggled to climb the fence manfully. Half-way up, she felt something tear, and saw with some annoyance that her shirt had ripped at the waist leaving her midriff bare. Ignoring a desire to give up her feeble attempt, she eventually got to the top, and straddling the fence hoisted over her leg to jump down. However, she lost her balance and fell ignominiously at his feet, on a pile of undergrowth. Luckily it was harmless undergrowth, without brambles, and she scrambled to her feet, brushing herself down briskly.

"Brilliant!" exclaimed Patrick, laughing slightly. "I couldn't have done better myself. Stiff upper lip, and all that!"

"Oh, shut up!" exclaimed Charlotte irritably, and thrusting past him began to make her way through the wilderness in the general direction of the sea.

It was not as easy a passage as she had imagined, and in no time at all she was breathless, and sweating profusely. Patrick was following behind her, and she turned and said: "If you were a gentleman you'd forge a way through for me!" pantingly.

Patrick grinned. "If you were a lady, I might just do that," he agreed. "However, you're at pains to remind me that you're here as the representative of Belmain Estates, a career woman no less, and as such you must realize you forfeit some of the niceties!"

Charlotte heaved a sigh, and ran a hand over her forehead. "Oh, please!" she begged, losing some of her assurance.

Patrick shrugged his shoulders. "All right. Move aside."

He brushed past her, and for a moment he was close against her, so close that she could see the tiny lines around his eyes, eyes that were still gently amused, and feel the warmth of his body against hers. Charlotte had an overwhelming desire to make him completely aware of her as a woman all at once, and not the annoying representative of the Belmain Estates. It was a temptation to which she almost succumbed, but then common sense asserted itself, and she decided she was allowing the heat and pulsating life of the island to get a hold of her.

Patrick soon brought her to the old Meredith house, a crumbling ruin now, overgrown with weeds and parasitic plants that had dislodged its timbers and thrust probing shoots into its walls. It had once been a bungalow, similar to the one Patrick Meredith now lived in, but now it resembled nothing so much as a derelict shack. The verandah had rotted into decay, a fair example of the way the jungle took back everything man attempted to take from it. Only the rambling bougainvillea and the trailing blossoms of frangipani added a touch of beauty to an otherwise desolate scene.

"Heavens!" exclaimed Charlotte, brushing back her hair from her eyes. The branches of shrubs had swept it into wild disorder, and with scratches on her face and arms she felt sure she must look terrible. "I'm sure Evan expected nothing like this!"

"Evan?"

"Evan Hunter. My employer."

"Oh, I see. Didn't Andrew explain the land would need reclaiming?"

"No, he certainly didn't. In fact, obviously, if I'd known what I would find when I came here, I would never have made the trip, to Manatoa I mean. I mean, even if Andrew had been here. I couldn't have stayed—*here*!" She frowned. "Your mother said that Andrew comes here from time to time and stays for a while."

Patrick kicked a rotting log aside, and thrust his hands into the pockets of his cotton pants. "That's right, he does," he agreed.

"But—I mean, does he stay here?"

"Sure."

Charlotte shook her head, and pushed her way through the shoulder-high grass to where the verandah steps used to be. She stepped over the crumbling woodwork of the steps, mounting a quivering plank which was all that was left of the verandah.

"Be careful!" said Patrick, indicating the shaking timbers. "It's dangerous! You don't want to bring the whole thing about your ears, or Andrew might charge you for a whole new dwelling." He grinned. "Get down."

"No. I want to see inside."

Patrick rubbed his nose with his finger. "Mind the spiders, then."

Charlotte gasped. "Oh, you beast!" she exclaimed. "Are—are there likely to be some?"

"Plenty, I should think. I don't think Andrew bothers to shift them. They probably keep him company."

"I think you're mean!" she exclaimed, but she pushed the door of the shack open very gingerly, throwing it back on its hinges, so that it creaked dismally, and a rustling among the dried leaves on the floor caused her to step back nervously, forgetting there was nothing to step back on.

She landed in the rubble painfully aware of a scrubbed elbow and bruised knees. She looked up at Patrick, and he helped her to her feet almost reluctantly.

"I did warn you," he remarked dryly. "Is that the end of the expedition today, Mr. Livingstone?"

Charlotte couldn't repress a smile, despite her aching knees, and said: "Couldn't we go through the trees to the beach? I'd like to see whether—well, whether—"

"Whether it's fit for development?" questioned Patrick coldly.

"Maybe." Charlotte bit her lip. "Now that I'm here, I might as well see everything!"

Patrick shrugged and walked away, pushing his way through the palms so that she had to run to keep up with him. When they emerged above an expanse of deserted beach, Charlotte caught her breath. Unlike the land, which was wild and desolate, the beach and the sea beyond had the same kind of beauty she had already admired near the Meredith house, Patrick Meredith's house. The palms swayed languidly in the breeze that lifted the waves into tiny breakers although as the reef surrounded the bay, it was not possible to make access by sea. How then did Andrew Meredith get here? Did he use the jetty near Patrick Meredith's house? It seemed unlikely. Then how?

Her mind puzzled this problem as she walked down the beach towards the water, kicking off her sandals and allowing the cooling waves to lap around her hot toes. It seemed yet another clue that there was indeed some other access to Manatoa. The thought filled her with anger. Obviously Patrick Meredith was deceiving her. She cast him a killing glance, but he seemed ignorant of her presence, standing lighting a cheroot with lazy movements, his eyes on the distant horizon.

Charlotte kicked the water impatiently. How dared he treat her with so little consideration? How dared he attempt to keep her here while . . . While what?

She frowned. What possible purpose could he have for keeping her here? After all, sooner or later Andrew Meredith was bound to return, and it was only a matter of time before the deal was put into operation. The delay was annoying, her indiscretions were infuriating, but not irretrievable.

Unless . . . She sighed, and looked back at him again. He always seemed so confident, so assured. He even treated her with indifference most of the time, and he of all of them ought to feel the most infuriated by her presence.

And yet he didn't. He treated her at worst like a precocious child who was attempting to play a game with her elders. Mrs. Meredith might act angrily, and make bitter, spiteful remarks, but Patrick Meredith had done none of those things. It was most disturbing. In consequence, when he said:

"Come on, it's time we were going," she ignored him, and instead paddled further into the water, trudging her feet through the coral sand, allowing its tiny fragments to slide between her toes.

"Miss Carlisle," he said clearly, "are you coming? Or would you like me to leave you here?"

Charlotte heaved a sigh angrily. She knew she could not allow that he would not do just that thing.

In consequence, she gave a particularly vicious jab with her toes before leaving the water to join him. However, as she did so, she felt a stabbing pain in the sole of her foot, and bit back a cry as it travelled up her leg like darts of burning steel.

"Oh, what next?" she muttered to herself, lifting her foot tenderly, and turning it over to see what she had done, wobbling slightly on her other leg.

She seemed to have cut her foot slightly, and from what she could see there was something embedded in the soft skin of her sole, just under her toes. "Damn," she said, trying to stand on the foot rather awkwardly. Whatever was she going to do now?

However, although the foot was painful, the first violent pain was subsiding, and she could walk on the foot if she limped slightly, and tipped the foot to one side. Hoping Patrick would notice nothing amiss, Charlotte hurried up the beach to where he was slowly walking back to the track to the house. Remembering the expanse of rough country they had covered to get this far Charlotte felt slightly sick, and wished she were alone so that she might sit down and endeavour to remove whatever it was that was embedded in her foot. But recalling the way Patrick had scoffed at her panic over the spider bite, she decided she would just have to bear it. She was probably imagining the pain anyway, as before. After all, it wasn't the first time she had cut her foot on the beach. When she got back to the bungalow she would use some of the antiseptic that Rosa had given her for the spider bite, and if she could clean it up without anyone knowing, so much the better.

Patrick turned as she approached him, and she forced herself to place all her weight on her foot so that he would notice nothing. But she had reckoned without the violent pain that again engulfed her, and with a helpless cry she sank down on to the sand, gripping her foot tightly.

"What in Heaven's name have you done now?" he exclaimed, half angrily, going down on his haunches and prising her fingers off her ankle. "Come on, you might as well tell me."

Charlotte shook her head soundlessly, suppressing a foolish desire to burst into tears. Patrick viewed her thoughtfully for a second, and then, seeing nothing on the ankle or the smooth curve of her foot, he turned the foot sideways, so that the injured pad could be clearly seen.

A deep frown furrowed his brow, and he said: "Did you do this just now? In the water?"

"Oh, yes," exclaimed Charlotte bitterly. "Yes, I know I'm a stupid creature—but it does hurt!"

"I'm not surprised," muttered Patrick, his voice harsh. "Charlotte, this has got to come out! It's a coral spine!"

Charlotte hardly noticed that he used her Christian name. But the word coral stuck in her throat.

"Is—is it poisonous?" she asked, endeavouring to sound calm.

Patrick shrugged. "It can be. Look, Charlotte, this is going to hurt you. Do you think you can stand it?"

Charlotte managed a tremulous smile. "Of course. Isn't that what any hot-blooded male would do?"

Patrick half-smiled, and then he said commandingly: "Roll on your stomach, and bite on this." He gave her a clean handkerchief, which she rolled into a ball, and pressed against her lips. She thought he was being unnecessarily pessimistic, and she glanced fearfully over her shoulder to see what he intended to do.

She could only see his back, then he bent his head, and she stifled the cry that sprang to her throat by thrusting the balled handkerchief into her mouth. The pain was agonizing, and she realized he had bitten out the offending spine, removing some of her skin in the process. He spat it out on the sand, then sucked her foot hard, arousing a pain almost as severe, so that when he stopped she lay exhausted, feeling completely enervated. She felt him bind another handkerchief round her foot, securing it gently, and then gripping her ankle, he said:

"You can turn over now," in a husky voice.

Charlotte rolled on to her back and lay looking at him shakily. "Thank you," she said inadequately.

Patrick's fingers were still resting on her ankle, and she wondered if he was as aware of them there as she was. There was a pulsing through her veins that had nothing to do with the pain in her foot, and the awareness of him she had felt earlier was now intensified by his touch.

"You were very brave," he remarked lazily, as she struggled to raise herself on her elbows. "I was afraid you might pass out on me."

He seemed to become aware that his hand was still on her ankle, for he looked down at it before moving to where she had turned up her trousers, and pulled down the cuff. Charlotte rolled on to her knees and got awkwardly to her feet, testing her weight on the injured one carefully.

"You won't be able to walk through that jungle,"

he said, getting up too. "The ground is far too un-
even, and probably infested with bugs. I'll have to
carry you."

"Oh, you couldn't possibly!" Charlotte exclaimed. "I'm much too heavy!"

Patrick smiled. "Well, we'll have to try it, anyway. Come on."

He lifted her up in his arms quite easily, and
Charlotte had to put her arms around his neck to
support herself. Then, ignoring her completely, he
strode back through the palms to the derelict
dwelling that had once been the Meredith house.
Then it became more difficult, as the shrubs closed
in on them, enveloping them in a twilight world of
greenery. It was getting quite late, and Charlotte
was sure that Mrs. Meredith would not be very
pleased when she learned where they had been. Nor
would she be likely to feel any sympathy for her
injury, for obviously had she not behaved so childish-
ly and carelessly it would never have happened.

Half-way back to the Land Rover, Patrick said:
"We'll have a rest," and stood her down on a dry
stump of a tree, some feet above the ground. Then
he lit a cheroot and said: "Why weren't you going
to tell me about that spine?"

Charlotte flushed, feeling quite ridiculous, standing up on the stump like an amateur on the stage for
the first time. "I—well, when the spider bit me you
made me feel so ridiculous, I naturally assumed you
would imagine I was making something else out of
nothing."

Patrick nodded lazily. "Okay, I'll accept that."

"Thank you," said Charlotte, with some sarcasm,
becoming aware again of the dishevelled appearance
she must present. For all Patrick had thrust his way

through the same undergrowth as she had done, and climbed the same fence, he looked cool and assured, even his hair lay thick and smooth against his head. She tried to pull her shirt straight so that it hid the midriff that the fence had revealed, but it refused to obey her fingers, and Patrick laughed at her efforts.

"Don't be alarmed," he remarked. "Women do wear less on the beach, you know."

"I know it," retorted Charlotte. "But whatever is your mother going to imagine has happened when she sees me? I feel an absolute mess!"

"Yes, you do look rather windblown," he remarked candidly. "Not exactly the cool detached Miss Carlisle you once were. But it suits you. I never could stand women who couldn't bear a hair out of place." He sounded smugly amused, and Charlotte felt angry.

"Did you put me up here to laugh at me?" she exclaimed, aware that her foot was aching quite badly now.

"Of course not. Why should I laugh at you?" asked Patrick easily. "As for what my mother will think of you, then I should imagine she'll give us a chance to explain before jumping to conclusions, as you seem to do."

Charlotte compressed her lips, and Patrick stubbed out his cheroot and said: "I suppose we'd better carry on."

Charlotte looked truculent. "I'll walk this time," she said stiffly. "At least that way I won't feel I'm presuming on your good nature!"

Patrick ignored her remarks, and stepped forward to grasp her firmly. Charlotte struggled desperately, but all she succeeded in doing was overbalancing so that she fell against him, and as his foothold was precarious among so many twigs and creepers, he lost his balance too, and fell back among the ferns with Charlotte on top of him.

"Oh, lord," she gasped, trying to struggle up off him. "I—I'm sorry!"

Then she realized Patrick was stifling helpless laughter, and became angry at his insensitivity.

"You are a brute!" she muttered, pushing against his chest in an effort to find her feet, but even as she did so, her eyes challenging his, she saw the laughter die in his eyes, and something else took its place, something that locked her gaze with his and caused ripples of apprehension to slide along her spine. "Patrick," she murmured half-heartedly, as his fingers slid caressingly up her back to her shoulders, drawing her persistently down to him again. His face was very close, his eyes half-closed and magnetic, and then with a stifled exclamation he pressed a hand behind her head, forcing her mouth to his.

Ignoring the agonizing pain that violent movements brought to the sole of her foot, she struggled violently against him, thrusting him away from her, and getting to her feet she scrambled breathlessly through the undergrowth in the direction of the fence. She was uncaring of the damage she might do to her foot, and even when he shouted: "Charlotte!" in an angry voice, she ignored him, and stumbled on. The fence almost defeated her, and she fell dizzily at the other side, shaking as much with emotion as pain. At last she gained the security of the Land Rover, and sank into her seat sickly. She wasn't sure what he had intended back there in the jungle, but he had little respect for her as a woman and her continual assertions of equality might have well been responsible for her losing what little respect she had left.

Swallowing hard, she fumbled for a cigarette, but the packet was empty, and she sighed heavily. Then she heard Patrick coming, and when he vaulted the fence and walked angrily to the Land Rover she wouldn't look at him.

"You're crazy, do you know that!" he muttered savagely. "Don't you know that infections are as easily gained here as bee-stings in a beehive? Dashing through the undergrowth like a mad thing! What did you think I intended to do to you?"

Charlotte wouldn't answer, and he flung himself angrily into his seat, turning on the engine with taut movements. Then he cast another glance in her direction.

"Did no one ever make a pass at you before?" he asked contemptuously.

Charlotte gave him a scathing glance. "You can hardly dismiss that—that—as a pass!" she exclaimed shakily. "Besides, if you imagine that by making love to me you'll deflect me from my purpose, you're sadly mistaken, Mr. Meredith!"

"Why, you—" Patrick said no more. He swung the wheel round, and the vehicle almost threw Charlotte out into the road, then he drove recklessly up the track towards the valley and the way back to the bungalow.

CHAPTER SIX

As luck would have it, Mrs. Meredith was not about when they reached the bungalow, and Charlotte climbed awkwardly out of the Land Rover and mounted the steps of the verandah with difficulty.

Patrick left the Land Rover in front of the house and sprang out too, going round to her side. "That cut needs dressing!" he snapped shortly.

Charlotte straightened her shoulders. "I'm quite aware of that. I can do it myself, thank you, Mr. Meredith."

"Would you recognize infection if you saw it?" he sneered.

Charlotte opened her mouth as though to speak, then decided against it. Instead, she turned and walked into the house with as much dignity as she could muster.

In her room, she sat on the bed and stripped off the handkerchief which was filthy now and torn. Then she limped into the bathroom and running some water into the bath placed her foot in it, making it as hot as she could bear it. The pain she experienced when she put her foot in the water was nauseating, but it eventually seemed to have the effect of numbing her foot so that when she dried it and smeared on the antiseptic ointment it did not feel quite so bad. She had no bandages, and rather than ask for one she tore up another handkerchief into strips and bound her foot up carefully. Then she stripped off all her clothes and bathed her body thoroughly, washing her hair and rubbing it vigorously to dry it. Afterwards she felt slightly better, although there was a vague sick feeling in the pit of her stomach, which she put down as much to nerves as anything else. Finally she dressed in the apricot tunic, slid her feet gently into her sandals, and glanced at her watch. It was a little after seven, and as dinner would be served shortly, she walked rather hobblingly along to the verandah. John and Michael were there, playing ludo, and they looked up as she appeared.

"Hello," said John. "You look awful. What's wrong?"

Charlotte sighed. "Nothing's wrong, John. I guess I'm feeling the heat, that's all. Where is everybody?"

"Well, Gran is in the kitchen with Rosa, and Uncle Pat went off in the Land Rover a short while ago."

"Do you know where he's gone?" asked Charlotte frowningly. She had an awful premonition that it was something to do with her, and she wondered whether he had no wish to set eyes on her again today.

Michael looked frowningly at John, and John nodded and said: "He's just gone somewhere," rather vaguely.

Charlotte sighed, and seated herself. Although the thought of food repelled her, the sick feeling was gradually dispersing, and she supposed in a matter of days her foot would heal as good as ever.

There was a box of cigarettes on the table, and she helped herself to one as Mrs. Meredith appeared.

"Well!" she said, standing with her hands on her hips. "So you got to see Coralido after all!"

Charlotte was glad of the cigarette and the

confidence it engendered. "Yes," she nodded. "It wasn't at all what I expected."

"I don't expect it was. Terrible waste of land, that is. Patrick never was one to take any notice of me!"

Charlotte sighed. "Well, at least I've seen it now. It's not very big."

Mrs. Meredith stared at her. "Do you think it may not be big enough for this development?"

"I didn't say that," said Charlotte quickly. "Naturally my boss, Mr. Hunter, will have the acreage already. He obviously thinks it's suitable."

Mrs. Meredith scowled. "You shouldn't say things like that—raising my hopes unnecessarily," she exclaimed.

Charlotte shook her head. "I won't mention it again, Mrs. Meredith."

Mrs. Meredith sniffed and walked to the verandah rail. "There's a storm brewing, by the sound of it. Can you hear that breeze stirring the treetops? That's the first sign."

Charlotte drew deeply on her cigarette. "You mean—a hurricane?"

The boys bounced on their seats. "A hurricane, Gran?"

Mrs. Meredith compressed her lips. "No, I didn't exactly say that, John. I said a storm. There is a difference. I think it will rain tonight."

Charlotte sighed. Obviously Mrs. Meredith was attempting to mislead her as she had apparently misled Mrs. Meredith.

The sound of the Land Rover returning brought her to the edge of her seat. The vehicle halted at the side of the bungalow, near the garages, and Patrick came striding across the lawns to the verandah.

Dressed in a dark silk lounge suit, he looked very attractive, but there was an angry expression marring his usually lazy features. He cast a cursory glance at the boys, then looked at Charlotte. His gaze travelled down her body to her feet, seeing the bandage she had applied.

"Well?" he said. "Is it all right?"

Charlotte nodded. "Yes, thank you."

"Good." He passed them and went into the bungalow, saying to his mother: "I want to speak to you. Now!"

Charlotte chewed her lips. Now what?

After several minutes, however, Rosa came to tell them that dinner was served, and the meal progressed quite normally, without any more whispered conversations. Charlotte felt strangely depressed. It seemed incredible that it was only three days since she had arrived in Manatoa. Already the people here seemed more real than Evan and her life back in England.

When the meal was over, Charlotte having almost choked on her food, Patrick did not wait for coffee, but shouted good-bye to them all and disappeared down the verandah steps again. A few minutes later Charlotte heard the Land Rover engine roar to life, and saw the lights disappearing along the path towards the interior of the island.

She felt absolutely exhausted somehow, and contemplated going to bed, but she knew she would not sleep. Conversely, she had no desire to sit with Mrs. Meredith, listening to her continual grievances. It seemed that Mrs. Meredith could not address her civilly unless it was to grumble about her reasons for being on Manatoa, and Charlotte had had enough arguing for one day.

She went to her room, found her foot was throb-bing again, and repeated the hot water procedure. Then she lay down on her bed and closed her eyes.

Although she had not thought she would do so, she must have fallen asleep, for she awoke with a start, hearing an unfamiliar thundering sound around the bungalow. It was raining, but such rain as she had never heard before, and the wind was howling like a thousand banshees. She could hear her shutters banging, and sprang out of bed, wincing in agony as her foot protested at such careless treat-ment. She closed the shutters, then stood for a moment to still the dizzy feeling the hasty move-ment had caused.

Then she limped back to the bed and looked at her watch which she had placed on the table beside the bed earlier. It was almost eleven, and she realized she must have slept for almost two hours. Sighing, she seated herself on the side of the bed, wondering whether Patrick had got home before the storm started. Surely she would have heard the sound of the Land Rover, although in her exhausted state she had fallen into unconsciousness almost without being aware of it.

Linking her fingers in her lap, she surveyed the crumpled state of her apricot tunic, and sighed. She might as well get undressed and go to bed properly, she thought, stilling the thoughts that plagued her mind; thoughts of high winds and heavy rains and hurricanes!

She undressed and put on her pyjamas, and the thin cotton wrap she had not bothered to wear so far. Then she unfastened the wrap again. What had she put that on for? There was no point in sitting waiting for the storm to abate. Sooner or later it would blow itself out, and there was nothing she could do to hasten that event.

Getting up again, she turned out the light, but as she did so there was a terrific crash almost overhead that seemed to rock the bungalow, and it was followed almost immediately by a vivid flash of lightning, that lit the room with its electricity.

In the normal way Charlotte took storms in her stride, but the kind they had back in England could hardly be compared to this violence. Shivering, she turned the switch on again, but this time the light didn't work. Shivering again, she flicked the switch several times, before realizing that something must have fused somewhere and the light just wasn't going to work.

Her hands felt clammy, and she felt furious with herself for feeling so nervous about a perfectly natural occurrence. However, she opened her bedroom door and stepped out into the corridor. Then she turned to the right, opening the boys' bedroom door, and peeping inside. She saw the two boys in another flash of lightning lying soundlessly in their twin beds, relaxed in sleep. Sighing, she quietly closed the door again. As she suspected, she was probably the only person awake, and it was bad luck that her foot should be so painful tonight of all nights, so that even had she wanted to sleep again, she doubted whether she would be able to do so.

The corridor was illuminated by another flash, followed almost immediately by one of those heart-stopping crashes, and she gripped her wrap closely about her, wishing herself far away from Manatoa.

Trembling, she stumbled along the corridor to the lounge, peering into the gloom fearfully, then drawing back with another gasp as yet another flash startled her. She waited for the thunder to follow, but instead there was a terrific gust of wind that sent the verandah door crashing back against the wall opposite her, and she pressed her hand to her mouth to prevent herself from screaming. A dark shadow loomed up out of the darkness, and she let out a small cry, before Patrick's voice said: "Be quiet! You'll wake the whole household!"

He closed the verandah door firmly, shooting home the bolt, and in the flash of lightning that followed Charlotte could see that he was dripping with water.

"You're soaked!" she exclaimed. "Where have you been?"

"To the generator," replied Patrick briefly. "What are you doing wandering about the corridors? Can't you sleep?"

Charlotte grasped her wrap tightly about her. "I was asleep. The storm woke me."

"Oh! Even so, why didn't you go back to sleep?"

"Because—well, because I don't like this kind of a storm. Is it—I mean, it's not a hurricane, is it?"

Patrick gave her a derisive look, then said: "Come into the kitchen. I want to get out of these wet things. You can make me some coffee. You are domesticated to that degree, I take it?"

Charlotte did not answer, but followed him down the corridor obediently. She didn't care how sarcastic or derisive he might be. She needed to talk to someone.

In the kitchen he switched on the light, and she exclaimed: "My light wouldn't work!"

"The generator!" he reminded her patiently, and she nodded understandingly.

"Wh—where does Rosa keep the coffee?"

Patrick indicated the percolator, and the tin of ground beans, and while Charlotte busied herself with her task, trying to ignore the shattering noises coming from outside, Patrick disappeared into his bedroom, emerging in a while in a white bathrobe, rubbing his hair with a thick towel.

Charlotte was intensely conscious of him, and when he leant past her to take his wet jacket and hang it in the utility room which adjoined the kitchen, she smelt the clean male smell of his after-shaving lotion, and the indefinable warmth of his body. She could recall with painful clarity the feel of his mouth against hers, and wondered if he had been able to forget that incident as easily as he seemed to have done. Then she thrust these thoughts aside and poured out two beakers of coffee, handing one to him, and cupping her hands round the other.

She was still limping, and Patrick said: "Let me see your foot!"

Charlotte shook her head. "That's not necessary. I—I've bathed it twice, and it's only sore, that's all."

Patrick shook his head. "I have no designs on you, Miss Carlisle. It's simply that I should hate to be held responsible for you if you should have to have yout foot amputated!"

Charlotte stared at him. "What a horrible thing to say!"

"Amputation is not a pretty word," he said shrugging. "Believe me, with coral, one can't be too careful!"

"You're trying to frighten me." She sipped her coffee and almost scalded her mouth as a crack of thunder overhead caused her to start in alarm. "Your mother tried to frighten me before dinner. She told me that a storm was brewing."

"So?"

"So naturally when I woke up and heard this terrible wind, I thought—well, I imagined, foolishly I realize, that it might be something else."

He gave a derisive shake of his head. "Charlotte's hurricane!" he remarked mockingly.

Charlotte turned away to add some cold milk to her coffee to cool it so that she might drink it and escape from his mockery. He had certainly banished her fears in the wave of humiliation that engulfed her.

"By the way," he murmured casually, "a certain Mr. Evan Hunter arrived in Manoata late this afternoon."

Charlotte was in the process of pouring the milk, and she swung round, spilling some on the draining board. She stared at him disbelievingly. *"Evan? Here?"* she gasped.

Patrick ran the top of his forefinger round the rim of his cup and raised his eyebrows. "Is that so surprising? It's what you've been waiting for, isn't it?"

Charlotte shook her head incredulously. "How—how long have you known this?"

Patrick shrugged. "Oh, maybe four—five hours," he replied indifferently.

She was astounded, and she sought one of the high stools that stood beside a breakfast bar, and sank down on to it weakly. Evan here, on Manatoa! It was fantastic! How could he be? And what was more to the point, how had he got here?

Patrick gave her a minute to absorb the information, then finished his coffee and replaced his cup beside the sink, ready for washing. He smoothed a hand across his damp hair and flexed his muscles tiredly. Charlotte, watching him almost unseeingly, suddenly realized that he looked tired, and as it was very late and he was an early riser, she was probably keeping him from his bed. But this information he had dropped so carelessly into her lap had stunned her, and she couldn't assimilate it immediately.

"Have—have you seen Evan yourself?" she asked at last.

Patrick nodded. "I had a conversation with him this evening, yes."

Charlotte gasped, "But how could you? I mean —you must have known before dinner that he was here; why didn't you tell me?"

"Because I wanted to talk to him alone," replied Patrick smoothly.

"And did you tell him I was here? Or did you keep that a secret too?"

"Why should I want to do that? You're not a prisoner."

"Am I not? You amaze me!" Charlotte was getting angry now, as realization that he had tricked her again became uppermost in her thoughts.

"Why should you imagine anything else?" he asked calmly. "I haven't prevented you from leaving the bungalow, have I?"

"Not much!" she exclaimed angrily. "There's a conspiracy here! I've said it before, and I'll say it again—' '

"Keep your voice down," he said mildly.

Charlotte seethed. "Well, where is Evan now? What have you done with him?"

Patrick raised his eyes heavenward. "I murdered him two hours ago, cut his body up into little pieces and fed him to the sharks!" he said in exasperation.

Charlotte glared at him. "That's not true!"

"No, but it's what you wanted to hear, isn't it?" Patrick gave an impatient exclamation. "Damn it all, what have I done to deserve this reputation, apart from reacting like any normal male when a young and attractive female falls on top of him!"

Charlotte felt the hot colour surge into her cheeks. "Did you have to bring that up?"

"Yes, I did! All this ridiculous outrage! Your precious Evan is probably tucked up in bed right this minute, enjoying a sleep, which is something I would like to be doing, believe me! He's staying with the Duprés, and tomorrow you'll both have a grand reunion, I'm sure!"

Charlotte bent her head, and heaved a sigh, and massaged her foot tenderly as the familiar throbbing began again.

"What—what did you tell him?" she asked, looking up.

"That's my business, *Miss Carlisle!*" He gave her a speculative glance. "Tell me something, though, what is your relationship to your Mr. Hunter? He's young, personable, and acutely anxious about your well-being. Could it be that he's going to be the answer to your maiden's prayer?"

Charlotte slid off the stool. "Evan Hunter is a married man. His wife has just had their first baby. The reason that he didn't accompany me here in the first place was because there were complications, and the baby was put into an oxygen tent. However, if he's arrived at last, then maybe everything is all right after all. I hope so."

"How touching!" remarked Patrick sardonically. "However, such complications are not necessarily a curb on a man's activities!"

Then before Charlotte could make any scathing rejoinder, he turned and walked to the door. Charlotte put out a hand.

"Just a minute," she exclaimed. "Is—is this Meredith man with him?"

Patrick smiled rather smugly. "Unfortunately no. But you'll have to wait until tomorrow for the details. I'm sure your Mr. Hunter will be able to answer all your questions. And now I'm beat—if you don't mind . . ."

Charlotte compressed her lips and limped across the room to the door, brushing past him, unwillingly aware that in spite of his attitude she still found him disturbingly attractive.

It seemed impossible that the morning should dawn so clear and untroubled after the furore of the night before. Charlotte, who had slept very badly, awoke with a throbbing pain in her foot, and a slightly nauseous feeling in her stomach. However, she rose and dressed early, impatient to see Evan to find out what Patrick had said to him. She wondered whether he had seen Andrew Meredith already or whether he, like herself, had arrived in Manatoa searching for him.

It was a little after seven-thirty when she limped along to the verandah to find Mrs. Meredith sitting there, having her breakfast. The sun was brilliant, reflecting the colours of the flowers that grew in such profusion around the verandah in prisms of light across the table. The air seemed acute and fresher, alive with the scent and sound of the sea in the distance.

Charlotte smiled at her hostess, hoping that

Evan's arrival would alleviate her situation considerably. But Mrs. Meredith merely said:

"Sit down. Rosa is bringing coffee. The boys told me you were in the bathroom a short while ago."

Charlotte said: "Thank you," and subsided into a seat gratefully. This morning when she bathed her foot she had found a patch of inflammation encircling the wound, and she had a vaguely heady feeling, which normally she would have put down to the heat but which now troubled her not a little.

Mrs. Meredith continued with her meal, then looked up.

"Patrick tells me you know that your Mr. Hunter arrived last evening!"

Charlotte nodded. "Yes. I understand he's staying with the Duprés."

"Hmm." Mrs. Meredith sniffed. "It's to be hoped this business can be finished with now."

"What do you mean?"

"All this ridiculous trouble Andrew has been causing. Maybe I ought to feel grateful to you. As Patrick says, if you hadn't arrived here so precipitately we would never have had the chance . . ." Her voice trailed away, and Charlotte frowned, only to realize that the reason Mrs. Meredith had stopped speaking was because a cream estate car was approaching the bungalow, and Charlotte got to her feet shakily, praying that it might be Evan.

But it was not Evan. It was Yvonne who slid from behind the wheel, smiling charmingly. Today, dressed in a red floral trouser suit, of light material, that drew attention to the slenderness of her figure, she looked rather sophisticated, and Charlotte wondered whether this unusual formality was for Evan's benefit.

"Hello, Mrs. Meredith, Charlotte," she called, mounting the steps easily. "Isn't it a wonderful morning!"

Charlotte sat down again, managing a light greeting, and hoping that Rosa would soon bring the coffee. Maybe the beverage would remove some of this sickly nausea she was desperately trying to quell.

"I thought you would be up early this morning, Charlotte," said Yvonne confidingly. "You must be eager to see your Mr. Hunter. He is a very charming man, is he not?"

Charlotte lifted her shoulders. "He is not *my* Mr. Hunter, Yvonne. But yes, I shall be pleased to see him."

"And I am here to take you to him," said Yvonne, in a very satisfied way. She glanced round. "Where is Patrick?"

Mrs. Meredith finished her meal, and wiped her mouth on a napkin. "He went out quite early," she said, using an entirely different tone of voice from that which she usually used to Charlotte. "I think he said something about going down to see Don. I'm not sure. I expect he'll be around to see you later."

Yvonne nodded comfortably. "*Oui*, I expect that is so," she agreed. "Have you breakfasted, Charlotte?"

Charlotte shook her head. "Thank you, I'm not hungry. However, I would like some coffee," this as Rosa appeared carrying a tray.

"Good, good. You have your coffee, and I will join you for a few minutes," said Yvonne. "Then we will go—yes?"

Charlotte nodded, and when Mrs. Meredith took charge of the coffee jug, she accepted a cup grate- fully. The hot liquid warmed her stomach, tem- porarily dulling the nausea. She couldn't understand why she felt so rotten, unless she was more nervous than she had believed herself to be.

Afterwards she followed Yvonne down the steps to the estate car, glad that she was not expected to walk far. Yvonne frowned at her awkward progress and said:

"What is wrong? You have hurt your foot?"

"It's nothing," denied Charlotte hastily. "Just a scratch!"

Yvonne frowned, shrugged, and then slid into the driving seat of the vehicle. Charlotte climbed in beside her, and waved at Mrs. Meredith who had come to the verandah rail to watch them go.

"Mrs. Meredith doesn't like me at all," said Char- lotte, sighing. "She blames me for the proposed development of Coralido, just as much as she blames Andrew Meredith."

Yvonne wrinkled her nose. "Mrs. Meredith does not live on Manatoa. Her feelings are coloured by her maternal desires for Patrick's future. She does not need to worry. Patrick is perfectly capable of coping with his own affairs."

Charlotte glanced at the other girl. "You sound very certain. Tell me, is there something I should know about Coralido? Or about Andrew Meredith? Do you know where Andrew Meredith is?"

Yvonne shrugged. "I might," she conceded slowly. "But if I did, I could not tell you. You will have to wait until your Mr. Hunter gives you all the details."

Charlotte heaved a sigh. "Honestly, this is

ridiculous! There's absolutely nothing anyone can do to stop Andrew Meredith from leasing Coralido to the Estates corporation! I don't know why everyone makes all this mystery out of it. It's a perfectly simple business deal!"

"Coralido is not my concern," remarked Yvonne lightly. "You must learn about it from someone else."

Charlotte twisted her hands in her lap, and gave her attention to the road instead.

The Duprés' house stood in the foothills above the village where most of the Fijians lived. It was of a similar design to that of the Merediths, with the exception of the swimming pool, which curved to one side, with the tennis courts beyond. A large outbuilding housed the doctor's surgery, joined to the main building by a covered footway.

Yvonne halted at the front doors which stood wide to let in the faint breeze, and slid out. "Come on," she said. "I expect Daddy and our guest are having breakfast."

However, as Charlotte mounted the steps with difficulty, a man emerged from the inner recesses of the house and came to meet them. Of medium height, and stockily built, with thick brown hair, and grey eyes, he looked so gentle and familiar that Charlotte, whose foot was really paining her now, felt like bursting into tears.

"Evan!" she exclaimed, with relief. "Am I glad to see you!"

Evan Hunter came to the steps, concern showing on his face. "Heavens, Charlotte, what's wrong with you? You look terrible!" He helped her into the coolness of the house. "What on earth has happened to you? Are you ill?"

Charlotte shook her head, and managed a half-smile. "What a greeting, Evan!" she said cajolingly. "You, on the contrary, look positively in rude health! Is Margaret all right? And the baby?"

"Sure, they're fine. Charlotte, do you realize it's almost two weeks since you left England, and I've heard not one word from you in all that time!"

Charlotte gave a helpless lift of her shoulders, aware that Yvonne was behind, watching them closely. "Can we go in and sit down?" she asked weakly. "You see—I've hurt my foot—" and with those words she passed out, falling helplessly to the floor at his feet.

CHAPTER SEVEN

For several days Charlotte was hardly aware of anything very much. From time to time she came round to find someone either tucking hot bottles around her because her teeth were chattering with cold, or at others placing cold compresses on her brow, which seemed hot as fire. But mostly she was unconscious of these ministrations or the people who administered them. Sometimes she would wake to find the bed soaked with sweat, and someone lifted her gently until clean sheets were restored and a cool gown was wrapped about her body. Once she thought she remembered Patrick's arms about her, but it was all mixed up with a dream she was having about their visit to Coralido and the way he had carried her through the jungle. Sometimes there was a pain in her head, an awful throbbing pain that felt as though it must split her skull apart, but then merciful unconsciousness would claim her again.

However, after six days and nights of misery, the fever left her, and one morning she awoke to find that the pain in her head was gone, and her body no longer burned her up. She was thirsty, so thirsty, and as she struggled up on her pillows she registered that she was in a strange room that she had never seen before. It was light and airy, and someone had already been in and slatted the shutters to prevent the sunlight from disturbing her. There was a jug of water and a glass on the bedside table, and she leaned over to pour herself some, only to find that when she tried to lift the jug it was too heavy for her, and in her frantic efforts to stop herself from dropping it she knocked the glass on to the floor with a shattering clatter.

Exhausted by the simple task, she sank back on her pillows, closing her eyes weakly. Then the door burst open and Yvonne Dupré came in.

"Heavens, Charlotte!" she exclaimed. "Are you all right? I heard a crash!"

Charlotte opened her eyes, and gave a slight smile. "I—I'm sorry, Yvonne, I—I don't seem to be able to lift the jug." She gave a deprecatory grimace. "I'm afraid I've broken the glass."

Yvonne came across to the bed and shook her head. "The glass is unimportant, Charlotte. How are you? Do you know where you are?"

Charlotte took a deep breath, unwillingly aware that any effort, even that of talking, exhausted her. "I—I suppose I'm a lot better," she said. "Have—have I been ill long?"

Yvonne shrugged. "Almost a week. You collapsed last week, when you came to meet your Mr. Hunter."

"He's not my—oh well," Charlotte sighed. "Am I still at your house, then?"

"Yes." Yvonne picked up the broken pieces of glass carefully.

Charlotte closed her eyes again. It was terrible feeling so weak and helpless. Opening her eyes, she saw that Yvonne had walked back to the door, obviously imagining she was going to sleep again.

"Could—could I have a drink, do you suppose?" she murmured.

Yvonne nodded. "I'll get another glass," and she went out, closing the door behind her.

Charlotte took another deep breath and struggled up on to the pillows completely. Then she looked about her. Apart from the door that Yvonne had gone out by there was another, and she hoped it led to a bathroom. Taking another gulp of air, she threw back the bedclothes and slid her legs over the side of the bed. The effort almost finished her, but she managed to sit up, on the side of the bed, getting her breath back. She wouldn't have believed such a small effort could make her so breathless.

She noticed she was wearing an orange shortie nightgown, one of Yvonne's, she supposed. Certainly it was the most ornamental thing she had ever slept in.

Then, as she was about to continue her efforts, the bedroom door opened again, and this time Simon Dupré entered. He was looking very doctor-like in a white coat over cream cotton pants, and he smiled when he saw her.

"Ah, my dear Miss Carlisle," he said, closing the door, and walking towards her. "I gather from my daughter that you are beginning to feel much better. Is that right?"

Charlotte managed a smile. "Thank you, Doctor, yes. I'm sorry if I've been a nuisance."

"Not at all. However, you've been an extremely lucky young woman. That injury to your foot might have cost you your life."

Charlotte pressed a hand to her throat. "Was that what was wrong?"

"Of course." Doctor Dupré took her wrist between his fingers and studied his watch for a few moments, and then nodded, satisfied, and let it go again, pressing his fingers against first one side of her temples and then the other. "Yes, you have had a fever, brought about by poisoning. Patrick told me you got a coral spine in your foot when you were on the beach."

Charlotte swallowed hard. "That's right."

"Of course, his cleansing the wound immediately saved you from a much worse infection," went on the doctor, putting his hands behind his back and studying her thoughtfully. "However, it was obvious that some infection had managed to penetrate even his ministrations."

Charlotte thought of the stupid way she had run away from Patrick, through the undergrowth which he had told her was dangerous, and felt the hot colour sweeping up her cheeks. This illness had been no one's fault but her own, and she felt angry and ashamed.

"How—how long will it be before I can get up?" she asked now.

The doctor frowned. "Oh, possibly tomorrow for a short while at least. You mustn't overtax yourself, as you will find you will lay yourself open to any other kind of infection that might attack your weakened condition. You're not causing us any inconvenience, believe me. I have a nurse, an Indian girl called Tara, and she has been taking care of you. As there are no other cases requiring her attention at the moment, I would advise you to take things very slowly."

"Oh, but—" Charlotte halted. "Mr. Hunter? Is he still here?"

"He is here today. He has been back to Suva during your illness to contact his business associates, but he is back again now. I expect you are eager to see him."

"Well, I did wonder what was going on," nodded Charlotte.

Doctor Dupré nodded. "Ah, here is Yvonne," he said, as his daughter came back with a glass. "Yvonne, tell Mr. Hunter Miss Carlisle is awake and wanting to speak with him."

"Yes, Papa," Yvonne nodded, and handing her father the glass she disappeared again. Doctor Dupré poured Charlotte some water, and while she drank it he said:

"Tell me, Miss Carlisle, is your foot troubling you at all now?"

"No. I can't actually feel anything, except the bandage." She looked down at her foot, and sighed. "I was a fool, and rather careless. Did—Mr. Meredith tell you?"

"Patrick?" The doctor shrugged. "My friend Patrick has been most concerned about you. In fact he seems to blame himself. Do you know why?"

Charlotte looked up. "Of course not. It was not his fault at all." She slid back under the covers and drew them over her. "I would think that both Mr. Meredith and his mother will be glad when I leave the island."

Doctor Dupré frowned. "And will you be glad, Miss Carlisle?"

Charlotte's colour deepened again. "Well, I—I have no feelings in the matter."

"Do you not?" Doctor Dupré shrugged. "Then of course I must accept your word. It was just . . ." He sighed. "Ah, here is Mr. Hunter. Come in, come in, Mr. Hunter. As you can see, our patient is much improved."

Evan came eagerly across to the bed, taking Charlotte's hand and seating himself beside her anxiously. "Oh, Charlotte, what a shock you gave

134

us! Heavens, I thought you were going to give out on me!"

Doctor Dupré smiled benevolently and went out, quietly closing the door, and Charlotte breathed a sigh of relief, gripping Evan's hand tightly.

"Oh, Evan," she exclaimed weakly, "it's wonderful to see you. I'm sorry I've been such a menace! You must be heartily sick of me."

"Don't be silly!" exclaimed Evan, looking at her intently. "You've no idea how good it is to see you looking more like yourself. When I arrived, and you collapsed at my feet like that, I wondered what they'd been doing to you. What a time you've been having! Why on earth did you leave Suva at all? And why didn't you wire me or something? I was half out of my mind with worry by the time I landed at Nandi!"

Charlotte lay back on her pillows tiredly. "One question at a time, Evan, please," she murmured shakily. "But first tell me about the deal. What's happened? And where is Andrew Meredith?"

"Andrew Meredith is in Suva," replied Evan, at once. "I saw him there yesterday."

"And the deal?"

"That's still in the balance. There have been complications. Look, let's deal with you first—why did you come here? And why did you go and blow the gaff to this cousin of Andrew Meredith's, Patrick Meredith!"

Charlotte sighed. "Didn't he tell you?"

"Well, I've had his version, yes. Something about your mistaking his identity. Did you do that?"

"Well, yes."

"But how? God, Charlotte, you knew that Meredith wasn't likely to be living on Monatoa in

135

luxury like this Patrick Meredith is, and still willing to give it all up to some development corporation!"

"I know, but Manatoa is a big island. And how was I to know that there were *two* Merediths?"

Evan chewed his lip. "That's a point, I suppose. Even so——"

"Even so nothing! Haven't you got more sense than to catechize a girl who's in the first stages of recovery after a severe illness!" snapped a furious voice from the doorway. "Hunter, don't you ever think of anything else but business?"

Patrick strode angrily into the room. He was dressed in slim-fitting pants that suited the muscular length of his legs, and a light blue knitted shirt was open at the neck. For once he seemed to have lost his normal control, and Evan got to his feet to face him equally angrily.

"Don't lose your temper with me," he burst out furiously.

Patrick gave him a derisive look. "Clear out of here! There'll be plenty of time for you to ask all the questions you want to ask when she's on her feet again?"

Evan stared at him in astonishment. "You can't order us about, Meredith!"

"Can't I?" Patrick walked slowly towards him. "Can't I just?"

"Oh, goodness, what is going on in here?" exclaimed Yvonne, entering the room and staring in some astonishment at Patrick and then at Evan. "What's the matter?"

Evan rubbed his hand over his hair impatiently. "Your friend Mr. Meredith seems to think he can throw his weight around," he said angrily. "Coming in here, telling me what I can and can't do. Might I remind you, Meredith, that Charlotte is my assistant, and as such, she is answerable to me for her actions!"

Patrick thrust his hands into his pockets. "What do you mean? Her actions? Are you referring to her mistaking me for Andrew?"

"You know more about that than I do," retorted Evan, his face pale with anger. "For someone who has such little compunction as to deliberately entice a girl to reveal confidences to you that you knew full well were confidences—well, I don't think you can criticize my methods!"

Yvonne's normally placid features were drawn into a frown. "Patrick!" she exclaimed again. "What is this? Surely it is nothing to do with you what Mr. Hunter chooses to say to his assistant!"

Patrick merely glanced at her. "Keep out of this, Yvonne. I know what I'm doing!"

Yvonne looked furiously at Charlotte, as though all this was her fault. Then she said: "Nevertheless, Patrick, you did keep Miss Carlisle here unnecessarily!"

Patrick swore softly. "Yvonne! Please!" He gritted his teeth.

Yvonne looked at Charlotte again. "You didn't know that, though, did you, Charlotte? If Patrick had wanted you could have left the island at any time he said!"

Charlotte's head was swimming with the unaccustomed strain of talking, and the disastrous effect this interchange was having on her nerves. But she frowned at Yvonne's words, and look at Patrick with questioning eyes. "Is that true?"

"Yes, it's true," said Patrick savagely.

"But how . . ." Charlotte's voice trailed away.

"The corporation, the Copra Corporation that is,

137

own a hydro-plane," said Yvonne, in a hard voice. "It's used in cases of emergency and sometimes for communication purposes."

Charlotte felt astounded. "But—but I never heard a plane—"

"You wouldn't. It's at the other side of the island," retorted Yvonne. "At Taiwanu. Isn't that right, Patrick?"

Patrick's expression was bleak. "As you say, Yvonne," he said icily.

"Well, she had to be told," exclaimed Yvonne defensively. "There was no point in keeping it a secret. Mr. Hunter could have told her himself."

Charlotte heaved a sigh. "I wish you would all go," she said tiredly. "I feel weary. Couldn't we leave this conversation until another day?"

Patrick turned, and without another word stalked out of the bedroom, followed rather anxiously by Yvonne, who seemed to be regretting her little outburst. Evan looked back at Charlotte, and lifted his hands in a helpless gesture.

"I'm sorry, Charlotte. I'll come back later as you say. Even so, I really think—"

"Oh, don't start again, please, Evan," exclaimed Charlotte chokingly. There was a tight feeling in her throat and she badly wanted to give way to tears. "Just go!"

Evan shrugged, and went out, closing the door behind him. Then she turned her face into the pillow and gave way to the hot tears that escaped from her aching eyes. After a moment she touched her top lip with her tongue, and wiped away the dampness from her cheeks with one hand. Why was she crying? What had she got to cry about? She ought to be feeling furiously angry. Patrick had certainly tricked her this time, keeping the knowledge of the plane to himself. And why had he done it? Obviously to give him time to complicate Evan's arrangements, but how could he have done that? Had he seen Andrew? Had he managed somehow to persuade his cousin not to sell to the Belmain Estates corporation? Charlotte felt confused with the thoughts that buzzed round her head insistently.

She pressed her fingers to her temples. She must remember, Evan was here now. It was his problem. If she had been the unwilling cause of his dilemma, then she was sorry, but there was nothing she could do about it. And after all, Evan hadn't seemed too furious with her, had he?

She sighed and closed her eyes. It was too soon after her illness to start worrying over such things. In that at least Patrick had been right. She was not yet ready to face all the complex tapestry of her work as Evan's assistant.

For the rest of the day she was left alone, apart from periodic visits from Doctor Dupré and his nurse, Tara. She liked Tara. She had all the calm, practical assurance of her race, and moved about her duties silently, conveying an air of tranquil competence. She wore European clothes, but her hair was dressed classically, and her eyes were long and slightly slanted, giving her a vaguely oriental air.

Charlotte slept a lot. She was still very weak, and the only food she could stomach was some soup and a little fruit.

The following day she was allowed to get out of bed, and she half expected Evan to appear at the first opportunity and demand his explanations, but he did not, and nor did anyone else. It was not until three days later that she saw a different face, and it was Yvonne's. The girl came in the early evening, before dinner, when Carlotte was sitting in her window, dressed in a light dressing-gown over her nightdress. Although she was growing stronger every day, and moved about her room and its adjoining bathroom freely, Doctor Dupré had insisted that she should not overtax herself, and consequently she spent many hours sitting at the window, watching the horizon where the sea flung itself into ragged shreds on the reef. Although she could not hear the sea, she enjoyed looking at it, and it soothed her thoughts into less chaotic channels.

Yvonne looked quite beautiful this evening. Dressed in a slim-fitting shift of cream lace that suited her dark complexion, she moved sinuously, making Charlotte overwhelmingly aware of the shortcomings of her own attire. She came across to where Charlotte was sitting in the light from a tall standard lamp, and said:

"And how are you feeling this evening?"

Charlotte lifted her shoulders. "Much better, thank you." She managed a casual smile. "I was beginning to think you'd all forgotten I was here."

Yvonne seated herself in a chair opposite, crossing her legs lazily. "No, we couldn't do that, Charlotte. But my father thought you had had too much excitement that first day you recovered, and advised your Mr. Hunter to leave you to recover completely before endeavouring to get information out of you."

"He is not *my* Mr. Hunter," said Charlotte patiently. "I told—Mr. Meredith—Evan is a married man, with a new baby. I'm merely his personal assistant!"

Yvonne raised her eyebrows indifferently.

"Nevertheless, it is easier to associate him with you. After all, you are in this together."

"I suppose so," agreed Charlotte quietly.

Yvonne got to her feet and walked to the window, looking out thoughtfully. Then she turned. "Have you seen Patrick again?"

Charlotte's eyes widened. "No."

"I wondered. He has been here once or twice to see my father when I was not here. I thought perhaps . . . But no matter." She smiled. "I'm glad you are feeling better. Soon you will be completely recovered, and then I suppose you will be leaving the island."

"Yes."

Yvonne nodded. "I must go. Patrick is taking me to the Perdoms. They are giving a party. It's a pity you're not well enough to attend. Your social life here has been singularly uneventful."

Charlotte's smile was a little forced, and Yvonne moved to the door. "By the way, you aren't the newest arrival here any longer. The governess Patrick hired in Suva—for John and Michael, you know—she has arrived. Her name is Virginia Lawson. She seems very nice. I expect Mrs. Meredith will be glad of her help. I hear, though, that Andrea and Simon are making an effort to patch things up. I wouldn't want the boys around when—well, when I go to live at the bungalow." She opened the door, and waved an elegant hand before going out and leaving Charlotte alone with her thoughts.

The next morning Charlotte asked Tara if she could get dressed. The Indian girl studied her for a moment, then smiled. "I don't see why not. So long as you just move around the bungalow, and don't make any attempts to go swimming or play tennis or do anything ridiculous like that."

Charlotte smiled, "I'm not completely stupid." She slid out of bed, allowing Tara to lift her foot and strip off the elastic dressing which was all that covered her injured foot now. "Can I see?" she asked.

Tara nodded, and went away to get a clean dressing while Charlotte lifted her foot and looked at its sole. The cut was healed now, and there was none of the inflammation which had caused such trouble. In England it would have been considered completely cured, but here they took no chances of a counter-infection, and the dressing would stay on for some time yet.

The only clothes she had to wear were the slacks and blouse she had been wearing the morning of her arrival. But they had been freshly laundered and felt good after wearing nightdresses for so long. Her hair was lank, and needed washing, but she had to be content with brushing it thoroughly until it shone, then fastening it back with a wide band of ribbon which Tara supplied for her.

She felt a sense of nervousness when she emerged from the bedroom for the first time. Tara directed her to the lounge, but it was all so strange; she still felt rather disorientated, though nothing was quite real. She supposed that was because she had been injected with so many drugs that she was not yet used to operating without any assistance.

As it was already after ten o'clock, she had expected to meet someone, but the lounge was deserted, and when a dark-skinned maid appeared, Charlotte asked:

"Is Doctor Dupré about?"

142

The maid shook her head. "He is in the surgery, Miss Carlyle," she replied. "Miss Yvonne is in the swimming pool, though. Would you like me to ask her to come here?"

"Oh, no, thank you." Charlotte shook her head. "It's all right. I—I'll just sit here for a while. Is Mr. Hunter not up yet?"

"Mr. Hunter?" The maid frowned. "Mr. Hunter is not here, Miss Carlisle. He got an urgent message from Suva yesterday evening, and he left early this morning."

Charlotte frowned. "Oh! Do you happen to know when he is expected back?"

"I'm sorry, miss, no. Maybe Miss Yvonne would know. Shall I ask her?"

"No!" Charlotte was quick to reject this suggestion. "No, it's all right. I'll find out later."

"Yes, miss. Is there anything else you want?"

"Nothing, thank you."

The maid departed about her duties, and Charlotte sat down on a low couch, flicking idly through a magazine. She felt restless, and she wondered whether she ought to risk Tara's anger and venture outside. It was such a beautiful day, and she had been indoors for so long.

She rose to her feet again and walked to the windows that overlooked the swimming pool. She could see Yvonne there, lying on an airbed beside the pool, shaded by a wide striped beach umbrella. Her body was tanned a deep brown, whereas the tan Charlotte had acquired before her illness had mostly disappeared. Her skin was barely honey-coloured now, and she longed to get out in the fresh air, and dispel the languor of the sick room.

The sound of a vehicle made her draw back behind the curtains, unwilling to be seen by any visitors Yvonne might have. It was the Land Rover that halted near the pool, and Patrick sprang out looking lean and powerful, dressed in denim jeans in a beige colour, and a cream denim shirt.

Immediately Yvonne levered herself into a sitting position, wrapping her arms about her up-drawn knees, smiling at him welcomingly. She had tied her hair up in a ponytail and looked young and vigorously healthy. Charlotte wrinkled her nose, hating the idea that she was witnessing a scene that was not for her eyes, and turning back into the room, she flung herself back on to the couch, moodily picking up the magazine again.

Obviously he and Yvonne were still on the best of terms despite the way she had betrayed his reasons for keeping the hydro-plane a guarded secret. Not that it had mattered any longer. Charlotte would have found out sooner or later from Evan himself, for obviously he had used some like method to reach the island himself. Why hadn't she thought of that? She supposed it was possible to hire a hydro-plane here as one would charter an aircraft in England. Apparently there were a lot of things she had not thought of, and she realized with a sense of loss that the job she had so eagerly taken on was rapidly losing its importance. She didn't know why, but here on Manatoa, the hectic life she led in England seemed soul-destroying and pointless. It was as well she would be leaving soon. England and the Hunter Agency were her life, and she could not escape from that fact.

Steps in the hall outside caused her to stiffen automatically, but she was unprepared for the angry exclamation Patrick made when he saw her.

"What the hell are you doing here?" he exclaimed. "You should be resting!"

Charlotte slid her legs to the ground, and got unsteadily to her feet. "I'm perfectly all right now, Mr. Meredith," she replied carefully. "Tara said I might get up today, and get dressed so long as I stay inside the bungalow."

Patrick glanced round at Yvonne who had gone to collect a towelling wrap, and who was now entering the lounge behind him. "Did you know Charlotte was up?"

Yvonne shook her head, frowning. "Of course not. How are you feeling, Charlotte?"

Charlotte compressed her lips for a moment. "I'm fine, thank you. Er—the maid told me Mr. Hunter has left for Suva today. Do you know when he will be back?"

Patrick's eyes darkened. "I have no idea," he said shortly. "Why do you want to know?"

Charlotte spread her hands expressively. "Well, naturally, when he returns, I hope to leave. I—I've presumed upon your hospitality long enough."

Patrick drew out his cheroots, then he glanced at Yvonne. "Get us some coffee, Yvonne," he said persuasively. "Do you mind?"

Yvonne raised her eyebrows indifferently. "As you say, Patrick," she remarked, and turned and walked out of the room.

After she had gone, Patrick said: "Sit down. You look as though if you don't you're going to fall down!"

"Thank you!" exclaimed Charlotte, somewhat

angrily, but she subsided on to the couch almost gladly.

Patrick lit his cheroot, then paced the room restlessly. He turned back to Charlotte and said: "You realize that if this Hunter chap returns in the immediate future, you won't be fit to travel with him!"

Charlotte's eyes widened. "Travelling isn't going to harm me!" she gasped. "Besides, I'm fully recovered. And before you say I told you so, I'll admit, it was all my fault." She turned her head away, looking broodingly at her fingernails.

Patrick gave an exasperated gesture. "You're very touchy!"

"Touchy? *Touchy?*" Charlotte glared at him. "Haven't I every reason to be touchy, as you so charmingly put it? My goodness, did you expect me to feel pleased that you've made a complete fool of me, making Evan imagine I'm some kind of incompetent idiot!"

"Because you inadvertently told me about the deal?"

"Because you *deceived* me into telling you about the deal, you mean!" she snapped. "And that was only part of it, wasn't it? Somehow you've used that information to complicate matters, no doubt using the very means of transport you denied there was!"

Patrick drew on his cheroot deeply. "All's fair in love and war, so they say," he retorted.

"And this is war, I suppose!"

"Right!"

"You're despicable, do you know that!" she stormed. "I don't think I've ever despised anyone as I despise you!"

"Why? Was the job so important to you?"

Charlotte bent her head, breathing swiftly. "It's not only the job," she said impatiently.

"Then what else? You're not going to try and tell me that this development would have been good for the island, are you? Don't you have any idea what commercialization does to a place like Manatoa?" Patrick paced about the room, smoking furiously. "Here, believe it or not, the people are happy. They enjoy their lives. There's little entertainment as you know it, but they have something that you and people like you will never have: contentment! You've no conception of the havoc that can be wrought by a group of slap-happy tourists, just out for kicks!"

Charlotte's nails bit into the palms of her hands. "You just won't try to understand, will you?" she cried.

"Will you?" he muttered savagely. "You're so wrapped up in your own selfish little world that you can't see the damage you might foolishly cause!"

"You know nothing about my world!"

"I know that it breeds sickness!" he said contemptuously, "mental sickness, of a kind we don't have here on our primitive little island! You don't hear of the islanders spending so many hours every week with their friendly psychiatrist!"

Charlotte couldn't reply. She supposed it would be easy to fall back on her condition, to pretend she was too weak to argue. But the awful trouble was that she could see his point, she could understand what he was trying to protect, and worst of all she admired him for it.

But because of this, because of this unwilling admiration that was rapidly extinguishing her resistance, she dared not stay here. She was no longer the objective representative of a business agency; she was simply a woman, caught in the web of a situation she had helped to create, and unable to extricate herself because her own emotions were involved.

In consequence, she turned on the one person responsible for this seemingly impossible state of affairs. Turning to look at him, she said:

"You don't care who you hurt, do you, Mr. Meredith? Just so long as your precious island remains intact. Well, all right, all right, I can see your point, but I deplore your methods." She compressed her lips for a moment to prevent them from trembling. "As for what you've said, you may know everything about your islanders, but you know absolutely nothing about me!"

Patrick stared at her angrily. "There isn't much to know, is there, Miss Carlisle? You're a pretty shallow person!"

Charlotte's fists were clenched into balls. "If I were a man, you wouldn't dare say that to me!" she gasped.

"If you were a man, things would be much simpler," retorted Patrick sourly. "It would give me the greatest pleasure to take you outside and take you apart with my bare hands!"

"Then why don't you?" she cried. "You've not shown any scruples before this!"

Patrick grasped her shoulders, hauling her up from the couch, holding her in front of him furiously. "One day you'll go just too far!" he muttered between his teeth.

Charlotte was quivering, but she would not give in. "Then what will you do?" she taunted him.

Patrick's face was very close to hers and his eyes, glittering with his rage, dropped suddenly to her mouth. His grip slackened slightly, and Charlotte's weak body leant against his for a fractional moment.

Then she was free as Yvonne came into the room, obviously aware of the tension, and of what she had just interrupted.

"Well," she said brightly, "here's the coffee!" She cast a malevolent glance in Charlotte's direction. "Did I interrupt something?"

Charlotte looked at Patrick, then rubbed her shoulder where his fingers had bitten into her flesh. "No, nothing," she denied dully. "Your—well, Mr. Meredith and I were having an argument. You probably stopped it coming to blows!"

"Oh, why?" Yvonne's tone was forcedly light.

Charlotte shook her head, aware that she was shaking, as much from emotion as fear. "Would—would you mind if I went to my room?" she asked uncomfortably. "I—I'm sure you'd rather be alone." She stumbled to the door, but Patrick was there before her, barring her way. "Let me past!" she said tautly.

"Stop being such a fool, Charlotte," he muttered. "Come and have some coffee. I'm sorry if I was cruel!"

Charlotte looked up at him. "I hate you, Patrick Meredith," she said bitterly. "Now will you let me go?"

CHAPTER EIGHT

FOR the rest of the day Charlotte managed to avoid the other occupants of the bungalow. It was not difficult. Tara told her that Yvonne had gone off with Patrick in the Land Rover, and Doctor Dupré was busy with his patients. She ate alone in the bedroom, and afterwards had a rest as the unaccustomed exercise had tired her more than she cared to admit.

It was very peaceful in the bedroom, the shutters drawn against the glare of the sun, but although her body rested, her mind was as active as ever.

She wondered what had taken Evan back to Suva with such haste. Had he had word from the representative of the Estates Corporation? It was possible they were agitating for some positive action. After all, it was more than three weeks since the operation, which was supposed to have been such a simple thing, had begun, Obviously, the Corporation would be getting impatient at the delay. They might even have found themselves another location. It wouldn't be the first time a deal had petered out because of competitive offers. A company like the Belmain Estates Corporation were hardly likely to have placed all their faith in the Hunter Agency. Possibly Evan's contract had had a clause relating to other agencies; if so, that might account for his apparent eagerness to complete the deal.

She rolled on to her stomach, resting her chin on her folded arms, wondering not for the first time whether her incompetent bungling of his plans would result in her either being dismissed, or at least losing the privilege of acting as his representative.

She sighed. Why did everything seem to be going wrong? Ever since she left the hotel in Suva it had seemed like one disaster after another.

When she awakened from the sleep that had over-taken her, it seemed hotter than ever, and she slid off the bed and went to the windows to throw wide the shutters. Outside, there was a stillness, and in the distance the sea looked very calm and the colour of lead.

Frowning, she turned back into the room, and going into the bathroom she took a shower. Tara had provided her with an old pink cotton dress which Yvonne had discarded and which would be more suitable for evening wear than her jeans, and she donned this gratefully; it was much cooler than slacks. The skirt was a trifle short, as Yvonne was smaller than she was, but otherwise it wasn't a bad fit. Tara had told her that Yvonne was dining out this evening, but that Doctor Dupré had expressed a wish that she might join him for dinner, instead of eating alone in her room. Charlotte was glad to accept the invitation. At least with Simon Dupré she could relax and forget the myriad thoughts that plagued her tired brain.

They ate in the small dining room that overlooked the foothills to the rear of the bungalow. The doctor explained that the hills provided a natural protection against the onslaught of high winds as well as casting a cooling shadow on the house in the heat of the day.

"You are looking much better," he said, with some satisfaction. "I think perhaps tomorrow we might allow you to go outside for a while. So long as the sun is not too strong."

Charlotte glanced out of the window. It was dark now, but she could still sense the faintly ominous intensity of a storm brewing, and she asked: "Do you think there's going to be another downpour?"

Doctor Dupré lifted his shoulders. "It is the time of year. Storms can break with tremendous speed and velocity. We have grown used to them. There have been hurricanes, but we are luckily usually on the fringe of the violence."

Charlotte smiled and nodded. "I gather they don't frighten you."

Simon Dupré laughed. "Hurricanes? No, of course not. They are a natural enough occurrence. Oh, I agree, they can be disturbing, and the damage they can cause to livestock and crops is phenomenal. But they are something we in the islands have grown to live with."

"I've heard that certain of the natives believe they can foretell the coming of a hurricane," said Charlotte, frowning. "Do you think they can?"

"Oh, I am a great believer in intuition," agreed Simon, nodding. "There have been too many instances where occurrences match their foretelling for it all to be mere coincidence. However, I am also aware that if one continually foretells something, sooner or later it will occur, and then one's prophecy is considered supernatural—or extra-sensory perception."

Charlotte sipped her wine. "You make it all sound so ordinary—prosaic, almost."

"What would you have me say? That the great wind is the spirit of a vengeful god? That is what some of the natives say, you know. Where there is violence and death, there are always those who create mystery and intrigue out of it. In a more commercial state, it would be what we would call capitalizing on circumstances. The tourists lap it up. They like the supernatural aspect."

"I don't." Charlotte shivered. "But I'll admit you've removed some of my apprehensions. I wish I'd spoken to you before the storm the other evening. I shouldn't have felt half so scared if I'd had your philosophies in mind."

"Then I am pleased that I have helped you in some way, Simon laughed. "I must confess I find the minds of my patients so much more interesting than their bodies."

Charlotte helped herself to some salad dressing. "I shall be sorry to leave the island."

"You expect to leave soon?" Simon frowned. "Patrick did not mention this to me."

"Patrick? I mean, Mr. Meredith? What has he got to do with it?"

"Well, as your host—"

"My unwilling host," Charlotte corrected him hastily.

Simon half-smiled. "You think so?"

Charlotte flushed. "What do you mean?"

Simon shrugged. "It is of no matter. But I think you underestimate yourself, Charlotte. I may call you Charlotte, may I not?" She nodded, and he continued: "I would imagine any man would consider himself lucky to have you as his guest!"

"Oh!" Charlotte bent her head. "You're very gallant!"

"Why do Englishwomen always make deprecatory comments when they are paid compliments?" exclaimed Simon curiously. "I mean what I say. And believe me, when a man gets to my age, he means what he says!"

Charlotte chuckled. "You're very good for my ego."

"Then that is good, too. I do not like to see that wan expression you sometimes wear in your eyes. I feel you are unhappy, but why? Surely the fact that Mr. Hunter is not going to lease Coralido after all does not cause you such heartache!"

Charlotte stared at him, transfixed. "Evan is going to lose the deal?" she exclaimed disbelievingly.

Simon looked a little disturbed. "You did not know?"

"No!"

"Then perhaps I should not have broken it to you so precipitately. That is why he dashed away so urgently this morning. I understand that a representative of the Belmain Corporation is in Suva."

"Oh, no!" Charlotte's appetite deteriorated rapidly. "And it's all my fault!"

"Hardly that!"

"Oh, it is! Don't you see? Without me making a fool of myself, telling Patrick Meredith all the things he ought not to have been told the deal would likely have been completed in Evan's favour by now!" She pushed her plate aside. "I'm sorry, but I'm just not hungry."

Simon Dupré wiped his mouth with his napkin, and stared at her. "I think, Charlotte, you have an entirely misleading comprehension of the facts," he began slowly, only to be interrupted by the sound of a car halting outside the bungalow, and a few seconds later Yvonne Dupré came ill-temperedly into the room, flinging herself into an armchair and surveying Charlotte and her father with sulky eyes.

"Yvonne!" exclaimed her father, in surprise. "I thought you were dining out this evening!"

"So did I?" retorted Yvonne angrily. "But as you can see, we were both mistaken."

"Where's Patrick?"

"He hasn't come back," she said, tapping her fingers irritably against the arm of the chair.

Simon frowned. "He hasn't come back?"

"No." Yvonne reached for a cigarette. "I don't know why he's acting like this!"

Her father lifted his wine glass. "Don't you, Yvonne?"

Yvonne lit her cigarette, glancing at her father impatiently. "Stop trying to psychoanalyse me, Papa," she snapped. "Or Patrick either, for that matter." She got restlessly to her feet and walked to the window. "He won't come back tonight. If the storm breaks it would be too dangerous!" She swung round abruptly, fixing her gaze on Charlotte. "Evan Hunter should be back tomorrow; are you ready to leave?"

Charlotte glanced at Simon Dupré. "Of course," she said.

Simon got to his feet, showing the first signs of anger. "Do not speak to a guest in our house in that manner, Yvonne," he said quietly. "Charlotte is not fit to go anywhere, as you must be perfectly aware, much less contemplating the arduous journey back to England. She will be staying here for at least another three days!"

"No!" exclaimed Charlotte, and then flushed. "I mean—when Evan—Mr. Hunter, that is—returns, naturally I shall leave with him."

"I cannot allow that—" began the doctor, but Yvonne intervened.

"Naturally she will leave with her employer!" she exclaimed sharply. "Don't interfere, Papa. There has been enough trouble here caused by our so-called guest!"

"Yvonne!"

"Well, it's true," exclaimed Yvonne defensively. "I know it wasn't her fault that she was forced to stay here, that was Patrick's idea, but now that it's all fallen through, there's no possible reason for her to delay. Good heavens, there are doctors in Suva. If she needs to recuperate for a few days, she can do so there."

Simon Dupré looked apologetically at Charlotte. "You must excuse my daughter, Charlotte," he said. "She's overwrought."

Charlotte stood up. "Don't apologize, doctor; I understand perfectly. And I should like to leave—as soon as it can be arranged." She bit her lip. "I—well, I just wish I could have seen Andrew Meredith before I leave Fiji—to apologize."

Yvonne gave a scornful laugh. "Of course, you've never met Andrew, have you? Well, he's not far away at the moment. I imagine he's at Coralido, nursing his injured pride!"

"Yvonne!" Doctor Dupré's voice was harsh. "That's enough!"

Yvonne looked mutinous. "Well," she said coldly, "it serves him right! If it hadn't been for him, *she* would never have come here in the first place."

Charlotte felt the hot colour flood her cheeks. "Would you mind if I went to my room?" she asked the doctor awkwardly. "I—I'm feeling a little tired."

Doctor Dupré rose to his feet. "Of course, my dear, go if you want to. But don't let my daughter's rudeness influence you. She isn't normally so impolite."

Charlotte managed a smile. "I understand your daughter's feelings perfectly," she replied, quite calmly. "But I am tired."

"Very well, then of course you must rest. Goodnight, Charlotte."

"Goodnight." Charlotte included Yvonne in the brief smile she gave before leaving the room.

But once in her own room, her assumed tiredness left her, and she moved about restlessly, lifting things on the dressing table, smoothing the bed covers, twitching a curtain into position.

Evan was losing the deal! That was the most disturbing thing in her mind. It was no longer in any doubt. Evan had wasted his time and money coming to the Pacific, and now what would he do? She pressed the palms of her hands against her cheeks. But why had he lost the deal? What had gone wrong? It didn't seem possible that Patrick Meredith could have influenced his cousin not to sell. Surely if he had had any influence over Andrew he would have used it years ago to enable him to buy Coralido. So what else could it be? Had an old will been found, something that proved that Gordon Meredith had not intended to withhold the ownership of the island from his brother who had been alive at his death? *No!* That would have been too much of a coincidence, so it must be something else, but what?

She walked to the window, watching the huge moth that was endeavouring to break through the mesh and reach the burning heat of the light. The air was heavy and oppressive, and she felt as though she needed air.

She wondered where Patrick Meredith was. From the way Yvonne spoke it seemed likely that he had gone to Suva, as well as Evan. But they had gone on separate planes, and their actions could scarcely be connected. They had hardly been civil to one another the last time she had seen them together, in fact, she thought dully, it was the only time she had seen them together. By contracting the fever she had successfully banished any chances she might have had of redeeming herself in Evan's eyes. She had not even been able to tell him herself about the unfortunate mix-up of identities.

Strangely enough, her emotions were not involved in that affair. Her job which had always seemed so important to her had assumed smaller proportions somehow. Any feelings she might have in the matter were all connected with Patrick Meredith. Every time she thought of him her blood boiled with resentment. Never before had any man treated her as he had done. Perhaps the reason she had taken it so badly was because although she had met unscrupulous men before they had not been like Patrick Meredith. She had thought that by now she was capable of recognizing ruthlessness, but she had been wrong. And maybe, too, she had resented the way he had made fun of her, amusing himself at her expense. She would not accept that she had been responsible for his attitude, that her frail efforts at appearing cool and businesslike were doomed to failure by the very warmth and essence of her nature.

She sighed, pressing her hands to her lips as she recalled the quite different emotions he had aroused in her that day he had taken her to Coralido. Then she had been more afraid of herself than of him, running away from emotions she had not known she possessed. All these things had added to her resentment. She didn't want to be involved with anybody;

she didn't want to experience that feeling of dependence that albeit unwillingly she could not help feeling when he was near.

She moved away from the window. How marvellous it would be if just for once she could do something to anger him, as he continually seemed to be angering her. But there was nothing, of course. He held all the cards. He had even pulled off the most important coup of all; he had prevented the development of Coralido.

Coralido!

Her heart almost stopped beating as pure excitement gripped her. Of course, why hadn't she thought of it before? Here was a chance to exonerate herself in Evan's eyes, and also a way to destroy Patrick Meredith's smugness. What had Yvonne said? That Andrew Meredith was at Coralido! She should go and see him, persuade him somehow that there must be a way to solve the problem. After all, that was what Andrew Meredith wanted, wasn't it? Yvonne had said he was nursing his injured pride, so Patrick must have found something out, done something to prevent his accepting the terms offered by Belmain Estates.

She paced about, thinking hard. When could she possibly go to Coralido? Tomorrow Evan would be back, and besides, Doctor Dupré would never give her permission to go there if he found out. She bit her lip. There was only one solution, of course. She would have to go tonight. As soon as it was possible to leave without anyone knowing she had done so. It was fortunate that Patrick was still away. At least if her absence was discovered he could not come racing after her.

She sat down on the bed, glancing at her watch.

It was a little after nine. At ten the household would be quiet. Unless they were entertaining the Duprés did not keep late hours, Tara had told her that. So she must sit and wait, and when they were asleep she would take Yvonne's car and go. It often stayed out front all night, and there was no reason to suppose she would put it away this evening, unless the impending storm caused her to think of it.

Taking off her clothes, she dressed in the jeans and blouse she had worn that day, adding a thick sweater which she found in one of the drawers of the dressing table. It was much too big for her, probably belonging to Doctor Dupré, but at least it was thick and warm. She had no desire to contract another fever.

Ten-thirty came at last, and the house had been quiet for quite some time. There had been no sounds of the car starting up, and Charlotte was relieved to find it was still standing on the forecourt. The keys hung in the ignition. There were no thieves on Manatoa.

The sky seemed low and black, and there was no moon tonight. She hoped she would be able to find the way all right. But she had a good bump of direction, and the time Patrick had taken her to Coralido had been on their way home from the doctor's house, and Charlotte thought she could find the track without too much difficulty.

But the darkness was all-enveloping, and when she started the engine, which seemed to create a terrible disturbance in the stillness, she felt a faint feeling of apprehension. Still, it was no use being frightened. There was nothing to be frightened about. She was merely driving to meet a man, a man she should have met almost a month ago.

Nothing disturbed the silence of the bungalow as she drove away, turning towards the north side of the island. She felt choked in the bulky sweater, and managed to wriggle out of it after the first few hundred yards. She had not known the night could be so hot, even the sea seemed to have stopped its ceaseless churning. As she drove she saw that nothing moved in the glare of the headlights; every leaf, every petal, every insect seemed still and uncannily silent. She shivered. It was uncanny. As though she was the only person alive in a terrible dead world.

Later, as she approached the dip into the valley before reaching the boundary of Coralido, she heard the sea. It seemed louder than she had ever heard it before, great breakers shattering themselves on the reef, creating an eerie sound of their own in the stillness. She wondered why she had never noticed the noise before. Probably during the day the sounds of the birds and the buzzing insects, and the normal everyday movements of small animals, disguised the violence of the ocean.

She reached the boundary fence and stopped the car, climbing out a little nervously. It was all very well feeling keen and excited back at the Duprés' bungalow, and quite another to appear at a strange man's derelict dwelling at eleven o'clock at night and attempt to introduce onself.

But she purposely brought all her resentment to the fore, and before she had chance to think again, she climbed the fence and jumped down into the undergrowth. There was a small squealing sound as she landed on some soft furry body that almost unnerved her, but she hastened on, hacking her way through the undergrowth as best she could, in the light of the torch she had found on the parcel shelf of the car. She had panicked when she had first realized she had no torch, but obviously in these unlit and desolate regions, one couldn't go far in a vehicle without requiring the use of a light for something. Apparently Yvonne was well prepared.

Charlotte tried to keep to the slightly easier passage through the jungle which she and Patrick had forged some time ago. There was still faint evidence of their passage, and this gave her a little guidance. But when she reached the derelict ruin of the old Meredith house, she was horrified to find it was blank and deserted, with no sign of a light anywhere.

She brushed back her tangled hair from her face, feeling a terrible sense of anti-climax. A wind was getting up that howled through the cracks in the decaying woodwork and whistled through the palms that protected the house from the sea. Charlotte shivered uncontrollably. There was something weird and unnatural about a deserted house at night, and here, surrounded by the encroaching mass of the jungle, it was as though the living plant-life resented her intrusion. Suddenly her small attempt at playing Patrick at his own game seemed to have fallen flat, and she could have cried with rage and frustration and something else: a kind of hopeless longing for a fulfilment which seemed never to be hers.

She was therefore almost petrified out of her wits when hands seized her from behind, and a man's voice said: "Who are you, and what do you think you're doing here at this time of night?"

Charlotte gave a breathless gasp, and when the man allowed her to turn to face him she flashed her torch into his face, causing him to drop his hands to protect his eyes. He was youngish, younger than Patrick, she estimated, and perhaps slightly resembling him, although he was stockier, more heavily built.

"Get that light out!" he exclaimed angrily.

Charlotte allowed the beam to fall slightly. "Are you Andrew Meredith?" she asked, sounding more calm than she felt.

"Yes," said the man, blinking his eyes. "Who are you?"

"I'm Charlotte Carlisle. You were supposed to meet me at Nandi airport several weeks ago. Do you remember?"

Andrew Meredith gave an ejaculation. "Good lord!" he muttered in amazement. "So you're the lady representative!" Then he gathered himself. "But that still doesn't explain what you're doing here at this time of night."

Charlotte glanced round, flashing the torch over the derelict buildings. "Are you living here?" she asked incredulously.

"That's my business!" he retorted sullenly, and then, as though regretting his rudeness, he said: "There's a building at the back. It used to be a stable. It's still in pretty habitable order. I use it when I'm here."

"I see!" Charlotte sounded astounded, and he said:

"Anyway, stop asking questions, lady. What I do is no concern of yours!"

Charlotte stared at him. "You might at least explain why you weren't at Nandi to meet me," she was stung to retort.

Andrew Meredith shuffled his feet in the undergrowth, moving leaves that were caught up by the wind and whirled into flurries about them. The wind was getting quite strong, thought Charlotte uneasily, hoping this interview would not last too long.

"Well?" she said. "What happened?"

Andrew Meredith shrugged. "I was unavoidably detained," he muttered broodingly. "Dammit, Miss Carlisle, why didn't you wait in Suva? You had no cause to come here. You might have known that sooner or later I would turn up!"

Charlotte felt annoyance stirring. "Time's money, Mr. Meredith!" she replied coolly, brushing back her hair as the wind persisted in blowing it into her eyes. "Look, couldn't we go somewhere out of this wind and talk? I'm hoping that there's some way we can sort out this situation."

Andrew Meredith stared at her. "What situation?"

Charlotte sighed impatiently. "That's a ridiculous question. There only is *one* situation that involves both of us. That of your being able to lease this land to the Belmain Corporation."

Andrew gave her an incredulous look, then laughed rather bitterly. "Oh, Miss Carlisle, where have you been these last weeks? Living in wonderland! There is no situation! There is no lease! The deal's off."

Charlotte was holding her temper in check with difficulty. Here she was, out in the wilds of the jungle, with a howling gale beginning to whip round her body like steel lashes, and the sound of the sea breaking on the reef like a roaring mountain avalanche in her ears, talking to a man who had not even the decency to be civil.

"I know the deal's off," she said carefully, "but that's why I'm here." She gasped, and grabbed at the bark of a tree as a gust of wind almost blew her over. "I was hoping we might be able to work something out. Nothing is ever impossible!"

"This is!" said Andrew Meredith briefly.

"But why? What has Patrick done?"

"Patrick?" Andrew gave a short mirthless laugh. "Patrick has had to do sweet bloody nothing. It was all done for him."

"What do you mean."

"It's a long story, Miss Carlisle, and I don't feel inclined to tell it."

Charlotte gave an angry cry, holding her hair back with one hand. "But you've got to," she exclaimed. "That's why I've come all this way. Please, Mr. Meredith, I must know."

Andrew Meredith looked around him. "Look at it all," he said harshly. "Beautiful, isn't it? Acres of uncultivated wasteland. Abundant in everything but water!"

"Water?"

"Sure—you know, that wet stuff that comes out of a tap!"

"I know what water is," said Charlotte stiffly. "But surely there's plenty of water on Monatoa."

"Oh, yes. There's plenty of water on the island. There's plenty *here* for a family. A stream runs through the hillside and comes out just above the house. It's what my parents used. But for a development of the kind Belmain Estates are planning, there would need to be a much more adequate supply."

"Couldn't they build a reservoir?"

"Where? This tract of land is small. It's long and narrow. It's practically impossible to build any kind

165

of watershed without encroaching on land that would be required for the development."

"Couldn't water be diverted from the other side of the island?" They were almost shouting now above the force of the wind.

Andrew snorted. "Could you see Patrick allowing that? He doesn't want the development. Surely you've gathered that in your short stay here."

Charlotte grasped a wedge of wood. Her feelings were hopelessly jumbled. She couldn't understand why the realization that Patrick Meredith had only been indirectly responsible for the breaking up of the deal should make her feel so relieved. It was as though a load had been lifted off her shoulders. Evan could hardly blame her for such a situation.

Suddenly there was the sound of someone else moving through the undergrowth towards them, and Charlotte frowned at Andrew as he turned. In the frail wavering torchlight, Charlotte saw a girl, a Fijian girl, dressed simply in a sarong-type garment of flowered cotton, her curly black hair cut close to her head.

"Andy," she called plaintively. "Andy! What are you doing?"

Andrew Meredith gave an impatient exclamation. "Go back to the house, Vika," he said, in an angry voice. "I told you to wait there!"

Charlotte stepped back a pace. "It's all right, Mr. Meredith," she said tautly. "I think we've said all that can be said."

The girl reached them, sliding her arms possessively round Andrew Meredith from behind. "Who is she, Andy?" she pouted. "What does she want?" She caressed his neck with her lips. "I don't like being alone."

Andrew Meredith looked exasperatedly at Charlotte, who was endeavouring to stand still in the gale that was rapidly increasing in strength.

"Look," exclaimed Charlotte, relieving him of explanations, "I must go. They—they might miss me."

Andrew Meredith looked as though he might say something, but Charlotte did not give him a chance. She plunged away into the bushes, only to realize with annoyance that instead of taking the path to the boundary, she had plunged through the palms to the beach and was standing at the top of the rise that led down to the lagoon.

In the torchlight she could see the breakers cresting the reef, the wind whipping them up into a frenzy so that it looked as though the ocean was boiling.

Boiling! Where had she heard that expression before?

And then she remembered, one of the boys had used it to describe the sea in a hurricane! But this wasn't a hurricane. Not this gale force wind that seemed little stronger than a severe gale back home in England. Even so, the sight of the breakers rolling unchecked into the lagoon which had seemed so calm that day she and Patrick had visited Coralido was rather disturbing.

Even as she watched, a huge wave lapped greedily over the beach, surging up the dunes to where she stood, and sucking gurglingly round the root of a palm tree in its path. It was a gigantic wave, and it was followed by another, that seemed to be capable of reaching the spot where she was standing.

Thrusting back any kind of panic she might have felt at that unnerving sight, she turned and thrust her way back through the trees to where Andrew and the Fijian girl had been standing. But they were nowhere to be seen. Yet she had to warn them. If they were staying out back of the old Meredith house they could be in danger. If the tide continued to rise at the rate it was doing, it would be little time before it engulfed the whole house.

Staggering slightly against the wind, she pushed through the trees to the side of the building, shouting: "Mr. Meredith! Mr. Meredith! *Andrew!*" at the top of her voice.

But although the sound seemed loud in her throat, the wind seemed to lift it and throw it away, so that it was barely heard above the gale. She tried again, but again there was no answer.

At the back of the house she could see nothing but a mass of trees. It was ridiculous! They had to be here somewhere.

She was panting with the effort, and her head was beginning to ache a little, but still she plunged on, seeming to get more and more lost among the thickly foliaged undergrowth. All sense of fear of the jungle had left her, to be engulfed in the purely terrifying knowledge of the damage that the roaring ocean might wreak.

Exhausted, she pushed through some trees into a clearing, only to find herself near the beach again, and even as she stood there, breathless, tears of frustration almost bursting through her eyes because obviously she was going round in circles, a huge wave lapped about her legs, almost unbalancing her.

Turning back into the jungle, she shone the torch desperately. She had the awful premonition that

168

there was no longer any time to waste searching for anyone. She ought to be seeking cover herself. The sound of the wind was deafening, and its shrieking was shrill in her ears. Once she glanced round at the ocean, almost fascinated by its pounding and booming, marching almost relentlessly towards her.

Then she fled, thrusting aside the trees, resisting a force that threatened to lift her and throw her back into the ocean itself. And where could she seek refuge? She didn't know where the car was, and in any case this wind seemed capable of lifting it and tossing it about like a toy. She wasn't safe in the jungle. Although it provided handholds for her frantic passage, there were creaks and groans as though the wind was endeavouring to tear the puny trees out by their roots. Once a twig flew past her, narrowly avoiding hitting her, and she ducked, only to bump her chin on a jagged tree outcrop.

Once she heard a terrific crash, as though a tree had fallen in the gale, but mostly the wind in her ears blotted out all other sounds. She was sweating profusely and her hair was wild and tangled, catching painfully on every twig that blocked her path. But she seemed immune to pain, absorbed in her own attempt at suvival against a force stronger than herself.

Now she could hear a door banging loudly, its insistence coming through the storm to her tortured ears. She gasped in disbelief. All her panting trek had been in vain. She was back at the old Meredith house.

"*Oh, God!*" she whispered wearily. "*Oh, God!*"

She was exhausted, she knew she couldn't run any more. There was no strength left in her, or any fear either. She was too exhausted even for that. There

169

was only one course open to her. She must brave the storm inside the frail cover of the derelict building. At least, she would be out of the wind, away from the tearing, destructive force of the storm.

She struggled along the side of the building, held tightly to the rotting verandah rail, and jumped the empty space into the doorway of the building. The wind caught her as she did so, so that when she grabbed the doorposts to protect herself, it almost wrenched her arms out of their sockets. But then she was inside, uncaring of a thousand spiders, and the door was pressed to. There was a catch, a frail thing that she doubted would hold, but there were wooden cups at each side of the door as though at some time shutters had reinforced it so that now she looked about her desperately, trying to find something that would slot across the cups and give her a little more protection.

Although the building shook in the wind, its foundations must have been firm, for it did not seem in immediate danger of collapsing. At least she would have to take that chance. Perhaps the fact that the wind could penetrate its walls was an advantage. It put up less resistance that way, reduced the pressure outside the building.

But what could she use to reinforce the door? There seemed to be nothing. Then she looked down. Some of the floorboards were rotten with decay. One was even splintered and sticking up dangerously at one end. With trembling fingers, she forced it up, the splintering sound it made almost scaring the living daylights out of her.

She gave a shaky laugh at her nervousness, then carried the plank across to the door. It was longer than she needed, but it fitted into place, and with a weary groan she sank down on to the floor of the building, all strength going out of her aching body. She wished she had a cigarette. Anything just to still the terrifying sense of fatality that gripped her. The wind howled furiously, there were terrible sounds of crashing trees and splintering timber, and the overpowering pounding of the surf.

She prayed the sea would not penetrate this far. It seemed to be eating the island, devouring it with its strength. It was awful. If only she had stayed with Andrew Meredith! At least then she would not have been alone. It was this feeling of being the only person alive in the world that unnerved her.

CHAPTER NINE

SHE didn't know exactly how long she stayed there, huddled by the door, before the sound of heavy rain penetrated the other sounds around her, and the paltry roof of the building began to shower bits of clay and wood down upon her, as well as spots of rain, huge things that trickled down her neck and dampened her cheeks. She was forced to move to a drier position, unwillingly conscious of the threads of spiders' webs that brushed across her cheeks causing uneasy shivers to run up her spine. However long was the storm going to last, and how long would the unsteady building stand up to its force? The darkness was claustrophobic. She had had to turn out the torch light to conserve what light there was left in case of emergencies. Any minute she expected to hear the rushing waters of the sea lapping round the foundations of her frail hideout, washing the building and herself away in its savage ferocity.

As she sat there, she wondered for the first time whether the storm had woken Yvonne and her father, and whether they had discovered the disappearance of the car. If they had, they would be bound to go to her room first to see if she had taken it. And then . . . And then what? They were hardly likely to venture out in this to search for her. And sooner or later surely the storm would abate, and she would be able to make her way back to the car and home to the Duprés' bungalow. It didn't matter what recriminations were waiting for her. At least she had the satisfaction of knowing that she had done everything that could be done.

The wind seemed to be getting stronger now, and from time to time a gust seemed in danger of lifting the house from its foundations, only to be foiled by the draughts that escaped through the broken floorboards.

When an awful, frightening squealing scream sounded just outside the building, Charlotte's blood seemed to run cold with fear. There had been something unearthly about the scream. Certainly no human being could have produced such a sound. She got to her feet, and pressed her body against the door, as though by so doing she would prevent whatever it was that made the sound from entering the building.

She was shaking with impending fear, unable to think coherently, unable to distinguish one sound from another. All that seemed to sing in her ears was the wind, and she pressed her hands against her ears, trying to shut out the sound.

There was a rattling suddenly at the door, and a heavy sound as though someone or something had attempted to reach the threshold but had fallen between the broken planks of the verandah. Charlotte almost stopped breathing. No one, no human being, could be out there in this storm.

She pressed closer against the door, listening, but apart from a kind of heavy breathing sound that might have been the wind, she heard nothing. Then the latch rattled again, and when Patrick's voice shouted:

"Charlotte, are you in there?" she almost collapsed with relief.

"Y—y—yes!" she stammered, through chattering teeth, fumbling to lift the plank from its resting place. "Oh, yes!"

At last the door swung inwards, and Patrick vaulted the empty space between the planks, landing beside her, his weight almost overbalancing her so that she clung to him helplessly, stammering out explanations like a child caught out in some misdemeanour.

Patrick caught her shoulders, shaking her violently, and then he put her roughly aside and turned to secure the door again. Charlotte hugged herself tightly, scarcely able to believe he was really here after the nightmare she had experienced.

At last the door was secured and Patrick leant back against it heavily, surveying her with the light of the torch he had brought with him. It was a more powerful torch than her own, and she turned aside from its brilliance.

Patrick seemed absolutely furious, and well he might, she thought gloomily. He would have no compassion for the reasons that had brought her to Coralido tonight.

"Well?" he said, at last, when her teeth were beginning to chatter again. "I suppose you're satisfied now!"

Charlotte pressed the palms of her hands together. "Wh—what do you mean?"

"You certainly chose the perfect method of frightening everybody half out of their minds!" he muttered squarely. "Just what did you hope to achieve?"

Charlotte shivered. "I—I wanted to see Andrew Meredith!"

"Did you see him?"

"Yes!"

"Then what are you doing wandering around alone in *this*?" he snapped.

Charlotte couldn't stop shaking. "I—I—I was going—going back," she began. "I—I—lost my—my—way!"

Patrick uttered an angry exclamation. "You lost your way!" he echoed. "You must have lost your senses as well! This isn't suburbia, Miss Carlisle, this is the South Pacific, and this is no ordinary storm—this is a hurricane! Or at least it was. Luckily, Manatoa caught only the backlash of it!"

Charlotte stared at him in disbelief! "You mean—you mean—"

"I mean that you could easily have been killed!" he shouted furiously. "Even here, in this crazy hideout, you're running the risk of being crushed by any one of these trees falling on the building. What protection would you have had? Damn it, Charlotte, you'll never know the torment I've been through tonight!"

Charlotte swallowed hard, trying not to cry. "Don't—don't shout at me, Patrick," she said unsteadily. "All right—all right. I've been stupid again. But—but I had to see Andrew Meredith—I had to find out—"

Patrick clenched his fists. "And what did you find out?"

"Oh—oh, about the deal—and why it's fallen through. Nobody took—took the tr—trouble to explain—it—to me!" Her speech was punctuated by the gulps of air she was taking. Suddenly she seemed breathless.

"Did you give anybody the chance?" he snarled angrily. "Oh, all right, we'll go into all that later Where is cousin Andrew? Holed up in his stable somewhere? I suppose he had company. That's why

175

he didn't invite you to stay." His tone was sneering.

"How—how did you know?"

Patrick shook his head. "Never mind. I suppose I ought to feel grateful that he had. Didn't it occur to you that it was unorthodox and even possibly dangerous to visit a man you've never even met before at this hour of the night?"

"I don't know what you mean," she exclaimed. "This was a business matter."

Patrick looked derisive. "Oh, was it? And what if Andrew's methods had proved to be less than businesslike, what then? If the storm hadn't broken, you wouldn't have been missed until morning. Charlotte, anything could have happened to you!"

Charlotte turned away, trembling a little. "Well, nothing did happen, so there's no harm done," she said, shivering.

She felt him move and his breath fanned the back of her neck. "Isn't there?" he muttered angrily. "No harm, you say!" He swung her round to face him. "Don't you care at all for anyone but your own selfish self?"

Charlotte linked her fingers together against her chin. "Of—of course I do. I—I'm sorry if you've been worried about me!"

Patrick caught her by the shoulders, staring at her with eyes that seemed to devour her as the sea had devoured the beach earlier. "To say I was worried is the understatement of the year!" he muttered savagely. "I have in turns wanted to take a whip to you or make love to you! Do you understand me, Charlotte, because you'd better. I don't care about the storm, I don't even care much what the Duprés think, we're alone here and possibly in danger, and all I can think about is you!" His fingers slid up to

176

grip her neck, his thumbs tilting her chin so that she was forced to look at him.

Charlotte was quivering in his grasp. "How— how long will the storm last?" she whispered.

Patrick gave a muffled oath. "God knows! Why?"

"And no one knows we're here—alone?" she murmured.

"No!"

"Then why should I trust you, any more than you say I should trust your cousin?" she said tremblingly.

"I didn't say you should," he muttered, bending his head and finding her mouth with his own.

The kiss was hard and passionate, a culmination of the fear and anxiety he had suffered when he first found she had disappeared, and although that was all Charlotte knew it was, she found she could not help but respond, winding her arms about his neck and returning the kiss with all the aching fervour of emotion long denied. This was what she had run away from. She had known that day he had kissed her in the jungle, though she would never have admitted it, then. She was in love with him.

A sob broke in her throat, and she dragged herself out of his arms. "Don't touch me!" she said, through her teeth.

Patrick uttered a violent oath, and without another word he turned and wrenched the plank out of its supports and flung open the door. Even as he did so a blast of wind and rain burst in on them, throwing Charlotte back against the far wall with its intensity. And with the gust there came the high-pitched squealing scream that had unnerved her before Patrick's arrival. Patrick swung himself across the verandah, and in the light of his torch she saw a wild pig foraging away in the undergrowth. Charlotte sought desperately for her own torch. The darkness was terrifying now he had gone.

But when she found it the bulb was broken, for it would not work no matter how she tried. It must have been smashed by the wind when it burst into the room, rolling everything about in its fury.

Charlotte felt hot tears burning her eyes. "Oh, lord," she whispered, wrapping her arms round her legs and sinking miserably down on to the floor, uncaring that the wind was now tearing into the shack, battering itself against the walls like a wild thing. So absorbed in her misery was she that she didn't at first realize what was happening until a terrible creaking and groaning noise made her stare upwards uncomprehendingly.

The sky was vaguely lighter than the roof of the building, and in the gaps in the roof it seemed to be moving strangely. Then she realized what was happening. The building was gradually being destroyed. Any minute the roof was going to fall in on her.

Gasping, she groped for the door, staggering across the broken verandah, scratching her legs to ribbons in her haste to escape. There was an awful crash, and then another, then as she scrambled away from the building it slumped in on itself, causing a terrific threshing and crashing in the undergrowth. Charlotte knelt where she had crawled, feeling an overpowering sense of helplessness. Patrick had gone, Andrew and his girl-friend had gone. And how on earth was she going to get back to the car? She burst into tears.

Then, as once before, she heard Patrick shouting her name. He was almost beside himself with anxiety, that much she could tell, and as she stared uncomprehendingly she saw him reach the ruins of the house, and begin to tear the timbers aside with his bare hands.

"Oh, Charlotte, Charlotte," he was saying, over and over again, and she got unsteadily to her feet and stumbled across to him.

"I—I'm here, Patrick," she murmured chokily, and he turned incredulously.

"Oh, Charlotte," he groaned achingly, and pulling her into his arms he buried his face in the tangled mass of her hair. "I thought you were in there," he muttered. "I thought you were dead! Oh, Charlotte, darling, darling Charlotte, forgive me for leaving you. But I love you so much, and I couldn't stand you standing there, tormenting me, when all I wanted—"

Charlotte pressed her hands against his chest and tried to distinguish his face in the gloom. Gradually the sky was lightening, and as the rain began to slow, so also did the wind.

"You love me!" she breathed. "You love me!"

Patrick cupped her face in his two hands. "Desperately, Charlotte, don't you believe me?"

And miraculously she did!

A few minutes later, when they were still standing, wrapped in each other's arms, the sound of people approaching caused Patrick to raise his head. In the lights of the torches they saw Simon Dupré and Jim Ferris, and behind them came the Fijian, Raratonga and Don Perdom.

Patrick squeezed Charlotte gently, then put her from him as he went to meet the men.

"So you found her," said Simon Dupré quietly.

"Yes, I found her," said Patrick, endeavouring to regain his composure. "Has there—has there been much damage?"

"I think we can leave that for the present," replied Simon, viewing Charlotte with some concern. "You ought to be ashamed of yourself, young woman, coming out here on a night like this in your condition!"

Charlotte managed a faint smile. She still couldn't quite believe the truth of what had happened in the last few minutes, and she almost resented the arrival of these men, who would separate her from Patrick.

Back at the Duprés' bungalow, Yvonne was waiting, looking cool and beautiful in a jade green housecoat. She looked at Charlotte with scandalized eyes and said:

"Heavens, Charlotte, you do love to cause a sensation, don't you?"

Charlotte had come back with Doctor Dupré in his car, leaving Yvonne's vehicle to be collected the following morning. Patrick had taken the Land Rover, and she presumed he had returned to his house. It was incredibly the early hours of the morning, and nothing seemed quite real any more.

Now Doctor Dupré said: "Is Tara awake? Charlotte needs a bath."

"I can manage," exclaimed Charlotte, but Simon Dupré shook his head. "No, my dear. Tara is here. You're probably exhausted, even though you may not realize it."

In a hot bath, scented with jasmine, Charlotte relaxed completely. Tara had washed her hair and helped her to soap her aching body, pouring jugs of steaming water over her tired limbs.

Charlotte looked at her curiously and said: "How—how did Mr. Meredith know I was missing? I—I understood he was in Suva."

"He was. He arrived back quite late in the evening. Naturally he went straight to his own house. But when the storm broke, and the household was awakened, and you and Yvonne's car were found to be missing, Doctor Dupré insisted that he be told."

Charlotte bent her head. "And Yvonne?"

Tara shrugged. "Yvonne only sees what she wants to see," she replied. "It has been obvious to everyone since your illness that Mr. Meredith has been more than mildly concerned about you. Why, he even came and lifted you out of the bed one day to enable me to change your sheets."

Charlotte sighed. "So it wasn't a dream?"

Tara smiled. "No, it was no dream. Do you love him?"

She was so matter-of-fact, so normal, that Charlotte said simply: "Yes. Yes, I do."

When she climbed into bed, tiredness overwhelmed her and she slept soundly, without stirring for almost ten hours. When she awakened, refreshed, a little after eleven, she found it difficult to believe that what had happened the previous evening was not just some crazy dream. She longed to see Patrick with a desperate urgency, and she slid out of bed eagerly, showering and dressing as quickly as she could.

She had to put on the pink dress that had been Yvonne's, but that didn't matter. Soon she would be able to go to Suva and collect her own clothes. She longed for Patrick to see her in something really exciting.

But when she reached the lounge she found Yvonne there, talking to Evan Hunter.

"Evan!" she exclaimed. "You're back!"

Evan came towards her, taking her hands. "Yes, I'm back. Honestly, Charlotte, I think it's just as well that I am. Yvonne has been telling me about the furore you caused last night. What on earth possessed you to go and see Meredith for yourself? All that has been taken care of." He certainly didn't sound at all perturbed, and Charlotte frowned.

"And you're satisfied that everything has been done?" she exclaimed. "You don't blame me—"

"Of course not. I couldn't blame you for such a situation. Besides, the matter has been satisfactorily concluded for all concerned, so we can return to England feeling quite pleased with ourselves!" Evan grinned.

"Return to England?" murmured Charlotte wonderingly. "But—well, didn't Yvonne tell you?"

"What should I have told him?" asked Yvonne, with a puzzled frown.

Charlotte's colour deepened. "About Patrick, of course."

"Patrick?" Yvonne wrinkled her nose. "Oh, by the way, that reminds me; I have a message for you —from Patrick."

"Oh, yes!" Charlotte felt a faint feeling of apprehension stealing over her. "What—what is it?"

"Well, he had to leave, early this morning. Some business I believe he had to attend to. At any rate, he asked me to express his apologies to you, that he would not be here when you left, to say good-bye."

"To say good-bye?" echoed Charlotte disbelievingly.

Evan looked strangely at her. "Yes, that's right, Charlotte. We're leaving today. I thought we could return to Suva and stay there for a couple of days, see the sights and so on, give you a chance to recover completely before returning to London. There's nothing particularly requiring my attention there now that we've wrapped up this South Pacific deal—"

But Charlotte barely heard him. She was feeling a terrible sense of shock, of anti-climax, and although the events of last night had been real enough, Yvonne's words brought back that awful sense of incredibility.

She sank down on to a chair, and Evan said: "Are you all right, Charlotte?" in a concerned tone.

"Of course she's all right," exclaimed Yvonne hastily. "Er—Patrick brought her things over from his house this morning when he called, perhaps you could put them in the car ready to leave, Mr. Hunter?"

Evan shrugged. "Of course. If you're sure—" He shook his head. "Are you sure your father said she could leave?"

"Oh, yes. Unfortunately Papa was called away to an urgent confinement early this morning or he would have told you himself. All Charlotte needs is a chance to rest and relax." She smiled charmingly.

Evan nodded and went out of the room. Charlotte looked up at Yvonne. "Patrick was here—this morning?" she said.

"Yes, Charlotte. Quite early on. Naturally, he refused to allow me to wake you. You were exhausted. You needed the sleep."

Charlotte glanced around. "Do you have a cigarette?"

Yvonne smiled. "Of course." Then after it was lit, she said: "Charlotte, I'm sorry. I know how you must be feeling."

"What do you mean?"

"Well—" Yvonne sighed, "it was obvious you mistook the relationship Patrick shared with you. I did warn you—"

Charlotte exhaled furiously. "You know nothing about our relationship," she said swiftly.

"Oh, but I do, Charlotte. I know Patrick. I've known him a lot longer than you have. I know his susceptibilities. You're a very attractive young woman. I suppose it was inevitable that—"

"Stop it!" Charlotte bit out the words. She couldn't bear to discuss Patrick with Yvonne, however well-meaning the other girl might be. "You say Patrick left the island this morning?"

"Yes."

"Why?"

"I told you. He had some business to attend to. Mr. Hunter was here when he called. He can vouch for what I say. I understand Patrick has even redeemed you in your boss's eyes. He's found another location for the Belmain Estates Corporation—a deserted island, with all the amenities they require. I think he felt bad about fooling you."

Charlotte felt as though Yvonne was systematically tearing her heart to shreds. "And that's why he's left this morning?"

Yvonne shrugged. "No, I think all that was tied up. To be quite honest, I think he wanted to save himself the embarrassment of explaining away the way he has treated you. You know what beasts men can be—"

"I don't," remarked a lazy voice from the doorway. "Do go on, Yvonne. Tell me!"

"*Patrick!*" Yvonne stared at him as though she was seeing a ghost. "But—but I thought you left for Suva this morning!"

"I intended to. Unfortunately the backlash of the hurricane has damaged the plane. It needs repairing. I came back to ask Evan if I could share his plane."

His eyes flickered to Charlotte, who had risen unsteadily to her feet and was standing watching them. "Well, Charlotte," he said, "Evan tells me you're leaving. Is that right?"

Charlotte spread her hands in a bewildered fashion. "I—suppose so," she said unevenly.

"Why?"

"Why?" Charlotte shook her head. "Isn't it obvious?"

"All that's obvious to me is that Yvonne can't have given you the message I left with her this morning. Did you, Yvonne?"

"She—she gave me a message!" stammered Charlotte.

"But not the one I gave her," snapped Patrick savagely, crossing the room to where Charlotte stood, and ignoring Yvonne he bent and kissed her, his mouth hard and passionate. "Relax," he murmured, his fingers curving round her neck. "I love you!"

Yvonne gave an angry gasp and ran out of the room, while Charlotte looked up at Patrick shakily. "Were you—I mean—did you promise to marry Yvonne?"

"To marry her? Never! Listen, Charlotte, I have the boys outside in the Land Rover. Andrea and Simon are together again. They're in Suva. They wanted me to bring the boys to them. I would have told you last night, but I never got the chance. That's why I had to leave this morning. Did you think I wanted to? When I came here, and Yvonne said you were still sleeping, I hadn't the heart to wake you, so I left her with the message that I've just delivered. Thank God for that hurricane! To think if I'd left the island you wouldn't have been here when I got back! He pulled her closer.

Just then Evan came in, coughed rather uncomfortably. "It's all right, Hunter," said Patrick, releasing Charlotte rather reluctantly. "You're not interrupting anything at the moment." He smiled. "I think Charlotte and I have sorted everything out. She's coming to Suva with us."

"Am I?"

"Yes." Patrick nodded firmly. "I think it will be a good idea for you to meet your future in-laws, don't you?"

Charlotte gave an enchanting smile. "You haven't asked me to marry you yet," she protested.

"Haven't I?" Patrick glanced ruefully at Evan. "Never mind, we can remedy that later. Are you ready to go, Hunter?"

"Yes." Evan sighed. "I gather I don't have an assistant any more."

"You do not," agreed Patrick swiftly.

Evan gave a regretful smile. "To think, if Meredith hadn't have got himself involved with that Fijian girl, this might never have happened."

Charlotte frowned. "Is that—is that the girl I saw last night?" She looked at Patrick. "Who is she?"

Patrick shrugged. "Some chief's daughter. I understand Andrew was forced to marry her or something. A kind of shotgun wedding!"

"So that's why he didn't meet me at Nandi!" Charlotte lifted her shoulders expressively. "Thank heavens he didn't. She looked mischievously at Patrick.

Evan turned and walked out, leaving them alone for a minute. "About Yvonne," began Charlotte uneasily. "I feel awful!"

"Why?"

"I'm sure she loves you."

Patrick drew her to him. "Yvonne isn't ready for marriage yet."

Charlotte slid her arms round his neck. "Love me, Patrick," she murmured.

"To distraction," he replied huskily. "Don't you know that's why I kept you here?"

Charlotte traced the line of his mouth with her fingers. "It wasn't the whole reason, though, was it? You were determined to prevent me from meeting Andrew until you had had a chance to complicate matters!"

Patrick's smile was enigmatic. "All right, I accept that," he said. "I warn you, I can be ruthless when it threatens something that belongs to me."

Charlotte smiled. "Are you threatening me, darling?" she murmured, as his mouth sought the nape of her neck and she felt the slight trembling of his body against hers.

"Yes," he muttered, firmly putting her away from him. "What I have I hold, and that includes you! But just now there are two children and a very impatient agent waiting outside, and a wedding to be arranged . . ."

THE END

To our devoted Harlequin Readers:
Fill in handy coupon below and send off this page.

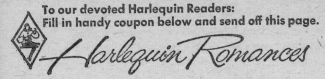

Harlequin Romances

TITLES STILL IN PRINT

51465 DAMSEL IN GREEN, B. Neels

51466 RETURN TO SPRING, J. Macleod

51467 BEYOND THE SWEET WATERS, A. Hampson

51468 YESTERDAY, TODAY AND TOMORROW, J. Dunbar

51469 TO THE HIGHEST BIDDER, H. Pressley

51470 KING COUNTRY, M. Way

51471 WHEN BIRDS DO SING, F. Kidd

51472 BELOVED CASTAWAY, V. Winspear

51473 SILENT HEART, L. Ellis

51474 MY SISTER CELIA, M. Burchell

51475 THE VERMILION GATEWAY, B. Dell

51476 BELIEVE IN TOMORROW, N. Asquith

51477 THE LAND OF THE LOTUS EATERS, I. Chace

51478 EVE'S OWN EDEN, K. Mutch

51479 THE SCENTED HILLS, R. Lane

51480 THE LINDEN LEAF, J. Arbor

MAIL THIS COUPON TODAY

~~~~~~~~~~~~~~~~~~~~~~~~~~